THE MATTER OF A MURDER OF A MAID

HADLEY SISTERS MYSTERY

A Novella by

Elizabeth A. Martina

Serra Books

An imprint of

Lanternarius Press
Oriskany, N.Y.

This story is a wholly imaginative work and, even if it contains references to real people, living or dead, the work is not meant to be a true story. Any similarities to real people is sheer coincidence.

Published by Lanternarius Press
Oriskany, NY.

Copyright 2020 Debra Booton McCoy

ISBN 978-0-9839758-7-8 paperback

To all the friends I left behind in Boston, a great city!

The Matter of a Murder of a Maid

TUESDAY MORNING

The telephone rang shrilly. Sally, the house maid, walked out to the foyer and picked up the receiver, answering, "Hadley residence!" She started as a screeching voice on the other end demanded to speak to one of the Hadley sisters. Immediately. She rushed the receiver and base back into the breakfast room.

Betty and Kate Hadley were already dressed for the day and seated at the breakfast table reviewing the morning offerings that Sally had just retrieved from the kitchen. They both looked up at the sound of the voice at the other end. They smirked and rolled their eyes.

"Evelyn Milton!" they said simultaneously and tittered.

"I will take it," Betty indicated to Sally, holding out her hand. Sally walked the long cord and base over to the table and handed the receiver to Betty. James, the butler and all around helping hand poured her second cup of coffee after refilling Kate's cup.

"Good morning, Evelyn" Betty began in her crisp business tone. She pulled the receiver away from her ear. Kate, on the other side of the table, could hear the shrill voice as well.

"Mary did not come back last night! How dare she disobey my orders. If she does return, I am going to fire her. No, I am going to kill her!"

Betty blinked at the receiver. "Mary? Your maid, Mary? The young one with the braids that she wraps?" As an aside to her sister, she whispered "The poor girl is so old fashioned!"

"Yes, that one! I have no other maid named Mary! I am just

beside myself. She is supposed to serve at my tea this afternoon! Now I have to find someone. Can I borrow Sally?"

Sally heard that and cringed. Her eyes opened wide and she shook her head slowly, side to side, silently refusing. Betty waved her off for the time being.

"Evelyn, don't panic. Perhaps there was a family emergency!"

"There is no family." Evelyn's voice was a little less frantic as she shared her worries.

"Has she a boyfriend?" Kate piped up, clucking her tongue in disapproval.

Evelyn heard and answered without Betty repeating the question. "She is just 17 and hasn't been here long. But I hear that the Italian chauffer for the Bridges has been eyeing her. Cook told me." Cook, Mrs. Kelly, who ran the Milton kitchen, could be a source of all kinds of gossip.

Kate leaned further forward across the table, but, before she could add a comment, Betty leaned away from her and waved her off. "Evelyn, dear, are you dressed?" Betty looked at her watch. It was only 9:00am. Evelyn was probably still in her dressing gown.

"I am. I was going to run out to have my hair done but Mary did not come down at 6:00 like usual. I couldn't give her instructions!" She was about to screech again.

"Stop it, Evelyn! And come over, now. You know our cook makes wonderful croissants. You love them." Betty banged the receiver on the base and motioned to Sally to take it back. She turned back to her coffee.

Kate looked at her timepiece. "How many minutes do you think? I say two."

"No. Three. She won't be able to decide on a hat." Betty looked

at her watch.

It was four minutes before James walked the upset neighbor into the breakfast room. Kate and Betty were on their second rolls and there were still a dozen left along with various other pastries and three types of juice.

Dressed smartly in a morning suit and a large felt hat, Evelyn Martin was the epitome of the spoiled, pampered Brahmin of Beacon Hill. She was disturbed that her day was not going right. However, it did not interrupt her appetite and she piled her plate before sitting.

"Now, Evelyn, please go over yesterday with us." Kate began. "Wasn't yesterday Mary's day off?"

"Let me see…Mary cleaned up after breakfast and set the table for lunch for two. Then she was to return to the house at 7:00." Evelyn took a bit of croissant with jam. "She did not return. Not last night. Not this morning." Her angst did not suppress her need to reach for another croissant.

"So you say that the Bridges' chauffer is interested?" Betty questioned. "Perhaps he may know something," she added.

"I am certainly not going house to house, interviewing my neighbors' servants like a common girl reporter!" Evelyn replied indignantly.

The girls looked at each other and pushed their chairs back. "Evelyn, why don't you go to your hairdresser so you will look lovely for the party. And we will call on the Bridges for you."

"We will help you find her in time for the party," Kate reassured their guest.

"Oh, you girls are wonderful!" Evelyn cried with a mouth full of delectable pastry. "But, if you don't find her by 3:00, may I borrow Sally? It is entirely too late to call the employment agency!"

Sally stared at her two employers, pleading. Betty smiled slightly. "Let's see what we find," Betty said to her in an undertone. Then she stood up. "My dear, Sally will get you anything you want. But, Kate and I have an appointment shortly and we have to go." Kate's head swirled around and she looked at her sister quizzically. Betty just went on, "Stay here, dear, until your appointment, if you like."

Then Betty turned around to the door. "Sally, have James bring the roadster around to the front."

The two sisters rushed out into the hallway, ready to burst with laughter. "Where are we going, Betty?" Kate asked in a whisper.

"We need to talk to that chauffer. It is 9:30. He should have returned from taking Mr. Bridges to work, but too early for a hair appointment for Mrs. Bridges. Get your hat on. Let's go." A swift view at themselves in the foyer mirror, a hatpin placed just so and the sisters were out the door.

The blue Mercedes Benz roadster was sitting at the curb, with the motor running. Betty got in the driver's seat and Kate got in the other side. The two-minute drive to the Bridges' house on Arlington was quick.

The sisters grabbed their purses and exited the car. They climbed the stairs to the impressive entry door and knocked. A young girl in a crisp black dress and white apron opened the door. She looked at the two.

"May I help you?"

Betty handed her visiting card. "Will you tell Mrs. Bridges that Elizabeth and Katherine Hadley are here."

"Yes, Ma'am," the young girl said, taking the card. She stepped

back from the door and pointed to the parlor, just off the foyer. "Please wait in here." The two sisters walked in and sat on French Provincial satin upholstered chairs. The Bridges were not chatty, sociable people. The girls had never been inside before.

It was only a minute before Aletha Bridges walked in. She was a small woman, impeccably dressed in a grey knit morning dress. Her hair did not need any help. Mrs. Bridges held out her hand and shook the hands of both sisters, then sat across from them on the couch, hands together.

"What can I do for you, Miss Hadley?"

"We are looking for a missing young lady."

"And how does that affect me?"

"We have heard that your chauffer knows her."

"My chauffer? George?"

"George? I thought your chauffer was an Italian!"

"Oh. That one. You mean Tony. I fired him last week. His accent. It is too strong. Mr. Bridges said it was too difficult to listen to."

"Do you have his address?" Betty asked. Mrs. Bridges face soured, but she got up and went over to her writing desk. She opened up a ledger book, took a small piece of paper and copied the address onto it. The woman walked over to the sisters and handed it to Kate.

"I do not want my name mixed up with some sordid details about a missing maid. Please do not release the source of that information." Kate nodded and put it into her purse. "I assume that is all you needed?"

Betty and Kate stood. They knew a dismissal when they heard it. They thanked her and left. The maid shut the door quickly behind them.

"That was not even worth turning off the motor," Betty mumbled, climbing into the roadster. Kate heard that and smiling, agreed. "So, my dear, what is this chauffeur's name and address?"

Kate pulled out the sheet of paper and read, "Tony Greco, 140 Parmenter, Apartment 3." She shivered despite the nice weather. "Not the most desirable address," she added with her nose wrinkled.

"Care to go for a ride?" Betty asked as she turned on the motor. "Hold on to your hat!" Betty rolled away from the curb towards Commonwealth Ave.

With the busy morning traffic, it took half an hour before the roadster pulled up in front of a beat up, whitewashed building in the North End. The narrow streets were not safe for the roadster to park, so Betty cruised a little ahead and found a small parking lot. They pulled in and walked the block back, the cobblestone street uncomfortable under their thin-soled pumps.

The front door was ajar. Betty walked in first, her spectator pumps clicking hollowly. The entranceway was empty, with only one door at the back, under a rickety looking staircase, sporting a cracked newel. She put her gloved hand over her hat, afraid of it getting covered with spider webs. Turning to Kate, who had stood at the threshold, Betty motioned her in.

"What's a little dirt?" she quipped stepping further in. Kate followed closely. Seeing no other approach, they went to the door under the stairs and knocked.

"Uno momento!" came a contralto voice, followed by two clicking sounds. Two locks! The door was opened by a middle-aged woman in a plain cotton house dress. "Si?" she looked suspiciously at the two young ladies, dressed in cool linen dresses, hats and gloves. They were obviously out of place here.

Betty was not sure the woman knew any English. "Does Tony Greco live here?"

"Tony? Antonio. Si! Up, up." She signaled, pointing up the stairs. "Numero tre. Three." She put up three fingers to indicate the apartment number, then frowned.

Betty smiled at the woman. "Thank you!" she said cheerily, wishing she had taken Italian rather than French at Miss Farmer's Academy. The woman smiled back and nodded.

The two sisters went up the stairs, refraining from touching the banister. The grime would never get off their gloves, if they did. One of the doors at the top of the stairs was marked with a broken tin numeral 3. The girls looked at each other and rolled their eyes. Betty knocked at this door, too. They could hear movement inside, but it took over a minute before they heard the door lock click.

A young man answered the door. His dark hair fell to his eyelashes and he swung his head viciously to get the hair out of his line of sight. He was disheveled. It looked like the knock had awakened him. The door opened only a foot. Their view into the room was fully blocked by his tall, lanky body.

"Ya?" was all he said, looking at them accusingly.

Kate piped up. "We are looking for Tony Greco."

"Who wants to know?"

"Well…" Kate began slowly. "Tony knows Mary Reilly, a maid for the Martins on Beacon Hill. And we are looking for Mary."

"I don't know nothing." He had a little accent but he was perfectly understandable. He stepped back as if to slam the door. Kate shoved her purse against the door jam, cringing at the thought of any marks appearing on the fine leather.

"Oh, no, you don't!" Betty yelled. She had no intention of his getting away that easily. She put her weight against the door and pushed hard.

The young man in question, lost his balance and the door flew open. The girls stumbled in, tripping over their heels.

"Pardon me! I didn't know I was that strong!" Betty blinked hard a few times, trying to adjust to the dark.

The young man, dressed only in a sleeveless undershirt and trousers, backed up away from them.

He felt behind him for his shirt, hanging on a nearby chair and pulled it on, buttoning it as fast as he could. He looked like he had had a rough night. The couch was rumpled and a full ashtray was on a side table. An empty chianti bottle was on the floor.

"Are you Tony Greco?" Betty crossed her arms, looking at him accusingly.

"Ya. But I don't know nothing about Mary. I left her last night and she was fine." He tucked in his shirt tails.

"So, you saw her yesterday afternoon?"

"Ya. We went to the Gardens." He turned to dig for something in the cushions.

"What did you do there?"

"We looked at the swan boats and walked around." He sighed with relief as he pulled a belt out from under a pillow.

Kate sighed back. It was difficult pulling information from this man. "You didn't go for a ride or anything?"

Tony looked down at his belt as he wrapped it around his waist. "Nah. I'm broke. No money even for a boat ride. I told her that sometime, when it's dark, I'll take her to sit on the boat and we can pretend we're going for a ride. But she had to get back early last night. That old lady she works for has her working on her day off! It wasn't at all dark at 6:30"

"Did you take her back to the house?"

Tony looked them up and down. "You got maids. They aren't humans with lives, like you people. You say show up on time or else. Right?"

Kate lowered her eyes. Yes, that was true.

"So, no. She was late. She had to run back." He buckled the belt and slapped the fake brass buckle.

"So, you just let her go back on her own?"

"Yeah. Sure." He eyed the pair uncomfortably. "Is that all? I gotta go look for a job. I got fired cuz my English is not so good." He barked out a disheartening guffaw.

"I am sorry we took up your time, Mr. Greco. We are trying to help a friend. That's all." Betty began to turn towards the door, letting Kate walk out ahead of her.

"Wait!" Tony took a step forward. "If you see Mary…." Betty turned around to look him in the eye. "If you see her, tell her I'm sorry."

"Sorry?"

"Ya. I'm poor. I got no business with a glam girl like her." The last sentence was uttered with regret. He turned away and walked over to the ice box. The interview was over.

The sisters walked back downstairs and out the door.

"Why don't I believe him?" Kate mused. They crossed the narrow street to the car lot, watching their steps to avoid the rubbish blowing around.

Betty nodded in agreement. "He is hiding something. Notice how upset he is. Too upset to be a guy who lost a girl he's dated only a month or so."

"Let's go see if Casey is in the office," Kate suggested. Lt. Casey Roach was Kate's man of interest. An up and coming police detective, Casey had neither the money nor the ethnic background to garner permission to date Kate, outright. But they seemed to run into each other often.

The ride over to the Sudbury Street precinct was quick in the midmorning traffic lull and they arrived well before any lunch breaks were expected.

"I'll get Casey to go out to lunch with us," Kate chatted. "There is a new darling little café at Scollay Square. He introduced me to it last month."

Betty pulled into a curbside parking spot just a block from the station.

"What should we tell him about our quest?" she asked. "Wait, I have to check my lipstick!" She looked in the rear-view mirror, licking her lips.

"I think we should tell him it's a missing person report. We don't have enough information to determine if Tony is involved, yet." They nodded in agreement and got out of the car.

They climbed the marble steps to the old police building and entered the foyer. The sergeant on duty at the desk halted them.

"Miss Hadley! You have to stop here, remember?"

Kate grinned. "Why, Mr. Ryan! How kind of you to remember me!"

"You here to see Lt. Roach?"

She tilted her head and smiled coyly. "You know I am."

Grabbing Betty by the elbow, she brought her forward. "And this is my sister, Miss Elizabeth Hadley. We both need to see him."

"Last time I looked he was in his office." Ryan was about to point then shrugged.

Kate was already walking away. She waved her hand. "I know the way!" Betty followed. Through the maze of offices and hallways, the clicking of their heels made heads turn. A few men even got up to poke their heads around the corner of the door jambs and watch the two walk away.

Tucked in a corner office, Casey Roach was

working on a report. His clacking away at the typewriter could be heard as they walked towards the open door. Kate walked up to the door and knocked loudly. Roach looked up, his face lighting up with a grin. He was over to them in a second.

"Hi, Kate!" He kissed her lightly. "Betty, how are you? What are you two doing here on a lovely summer morning?"

"I have come for advice, Casey," Kate began as she and Betty walked towards the old leather chairs.

"Then come in and have a seat. Coffee, water?"

Kate remembered that brown burned liquid the police insisted on calling coffee, and shivered. "No. Thank you. We need your help. We think we are on to a crime."

Casey looked down at her. "Kate! What did I tell you? Leave that stuff to me. You can find other interests."

Betty piped up. "You have to know it just rolled into our laps."

"And only this morning," Kate added.

Casey sat on the edge of his desk. "Ok, you two. Spell it out." It

only took a minute to bring him the highlights of the day's events.

"So, let me get this straight. Some teenaged maid did not return to a house last night and you are panicking."

"No. Well, yes."

"It's Tony. He seems very strange."

"Have you met him before?"

"No."

"Then," Casey pointed out. "How do you know that is not just how he is?"

The sisters looked at each other. They could not answer that one.

"Besides," the police Lieutenant added, "you cannot file a missing person's report."

"Why?" both sisters asked simultaneously.

"Because she has not been missing 24 hours yet." Casey grinned at their downcast looks.

"I tell you what. Call me after 7 tonight. If she still is missing, I will write up the complaint." He got off the desk. "I thought you had a tea or something this afternoon, Kate."

"Oh, we do. But we do not need much time to prepare. I need lunch, first." She looked up at him.

"I'm sorry. I can't help you there. We just got a report of a vandalized swan boat from the Garden this morning. We sent off two officers to investigate and I have to write up the report as soon as they return." He rolled his eyes. "I am stuck here." Casey looked apologetic.

"Well, then, why don't Betty and I go have lunch and we will bring you something when we are done."

"Gee, thanks, Kate. That would be swell!" Casey kissed her

cheek, walked them to the door and returned to his desk to resume work.

As the girls walked down the hall, Betty turned to Kate. "Did you hear what Casey said? A vandalized swan boat...."

"And....?"

"Didn't Tony say that he couldn't afford to give Mary a swan boat ride last night?"

"He did, didn't he!" Kate grinned mischievously.

"Kate, are you very hungry? I thought maybe we could go to the Garden and see if there are any police or reporters who wouldn't mind talking."

"There goes my lunch. We can pick up something for Casey at the Garden. A few hot dogs, maybe." Kate waved to Officer Ryan as they passed his desk and walked out the front door.

"You are a good sport, Kate! I just have to know. And, a picture is worth a thousand words. More so, if I can see the vandalism, myself!"

They walked the block to the car and got in. Betty wheeled out into traffic and down Sudbury. The traffic had picked up since they had been in the police station. She drove around the back of the Suffolk County Court House and made her way onto Beacon St, then pulled to the curb behind a police car. They could see a crowd of people gathered around the pond and raced over to join.

Two reporters, whom Kate recognized as being from the Herald and the Evening Globe, were standing by the two police officers, talking. Kate recognized one of the officers as being from the Sudbury St. station. She walked as close as five feet from him and smiled up at him. Officer Perkins caught her eye, looked down at her and tipped his hat. He excused himself from the reporters and stepped over to her.

"Miss Hadley, what are you doing here?"

"Oh, I am a little curious, Officer Perkins. My sister and I were just coming from the house and saw all this business. And, you know, we just had to stop and watch!"

"Well, don't say anything to anyone, Miss Hadley, but someone is in a lot of trouble. See that first swan boat in line, there?"

Kate craned her neck to see the boats sitting in the pond, 100 yards or more across the grass. "What am I looking for?"

"Well, you can't see from this far off, but someone managed to pull a bench off and break off a leg. I think the person must have had a hammer, judging from the marks."

Kate looked up in feigned shock. "How awful to do that to those darling little boats!"

Betty came up behind Kate after listening to the reporters ask questions. "Do you know who did it?" she asked with an innocent look.

"Not yet. But we will get our man," the policeman insisted. "Please excuse me. I have work to do," he added then tipped his hat and walked back to the other three.

"This doesn't give us any help," Kate stated. "Tony does not seem to be the type who would be walking around Boston with a hammer, especially not while on a date. Judging from his weight, I would say he would rather spend money on a hotdog than a construction tool."

They started walking along the grass away from the pond. Betty spotted a hot dog stand. "You did promise Casey lunch. And I need something to eat before that tea. How about a few hotdogs?" Kate walked up to the stand.

The man at the counter looked troubled. He glared at them.

"We'll take four hot dogs, two with chili, two without. And

three tonics," Kate ordered. The man nodded and turned away.

"How is business today?" Betty tried to enliven the man.

"See all these cops?" he said pointing with his chin. "Bad for business. No mother is going to let her little kid go on a swan boat ride with cops and reporters prowling around. Same as last night."

Betty and Kate's ears pricked up. "Last night? What happened last night?"

"Some guys got into a fight. A girl was screaming. I couldn't get one tonic sold with all the shenanigans. And I am usually pretty busy at closing. Everyone wants one more tonic before heading home."

The sisters looked at each other knowingly. "Did you see the men?"

"Nah. They were the other side of the boathouse. All I heard was the yelling."

Betty's shoulders fell with that piece of news. Kate

asked, "Weren't there late boat riders who would have seen something?"

"Nah. Boat rides close hours before the Gardens close. This way the boats are cleaned up and put away before then." He handed the hotdogs and drinks to the girls in a box. "You are my best sale all day." He grinned a little.

The girls took the items back to the car. "I am working on a theory, Kate," Betty said, pulling out the key. "I don't think Tony and Mary parted ways at 6:30. And I think there was a third party involved."

"You can't say that this vandalism is somehow connected with Mary. Are you? I mean, there is no proof. Nothing."

"You know we will find it, don't you, Kate." Betty retorted, sliding into her seat. "Hand me the box so nothing spills, before you get in." Kate slid in and Betty handed her back the box.

"We may as well admit to Casey that we can't let go of this story. It is just falling into place," Kate commented as Betty pulled into traffic and went west on Beacon. She turned left onto Charles and drove the short distance back to the police station.

Armed with food, they retraced their steps and reported in to Sergeant Ryan. "We brought food!" they announced. "For the lieutenant!" They smoothly walked right past him and down the corridors to Casey's office. He was on the phone when they arrived and he waved them to the chairs. Kate separated the hotdogs with chili and put them on a napkin in front of him, then added his bottle of soda. The girls munched on their snacks while they waited for him to get off the phone.

Casey hung up the receiver and turned to the sisters. "Thank you for the lunch, ladies. But would you tell me how it is that you ignored my warning and went directly over to the Gardens?"

Kate blushed a little. That Perkins was going to get a piece of her mind. Later. "We just had to see what a vandalized swan boat looked like," she grinned.

Betty finished chewing and added, "You didn't say anything about looking at swan boats, Casey."

The lieutenant sighed and glared at the two. "You two are going to get into big trouble someday. And then I will have extra work trying to get you out of it." He shook his head and bit into his chili hot dog, chewing thoughtfully for a moment. "So, what did you find? You are both on edge. I know some-thing's up." He turned to Betty for an answer.

She wiped a drop of mustard off her lip and began. "When we went to see Tony Greco, he asked us to apologize to Mary, when we find her, for his not having money enough to take her on a swan ride.

That's one. Then, Mary lives only a few blocks from the Gardens, an easy walk to the swan boats. He said she went home from the Gardens last night at 6:30. She knew she had to be back at 7:00. Then, we were talking to the man who runs the catering stand. He told us about an argument near the pond about the time the Gardens were closing down for the night. Two men, he said."

"And a woman screaming," added Kate.

"Then you add on to that scenario the vandalized boat," Casey mused. He opened his bottle of soda and downed half of it. "It may all be a coincidence, but I wouldn't bet on it."

Kate looked at her watch. "It is after 1:00! Betty, we have to go get ready."

"I am glad to hear you have something important to do," Casey sarcastically pointed out. "I may get a handle on this missing person while you party your way through the early evening." The sisters laughed at his attempted joke. They rose, rolling up the wasted paper napkins and tossed it all.

Kate leaned over the desk. "Will you call me tonight?"

"Of course," he said softly, then, louder, he added, "Especially if I find more information for you junior detectives!"

Kate smiled, turned away and left, following Betty down the dark hall.

TUESDAY EVENING

The tea party at the Miltons' was the first since Evelyn Milton and her husband had moved onto Mt. Vernon St a year before. George Milton had married the widow Evelyn Gardner to enhance his entry into Boston upper crust society after attaining presidency of the Federal Reserve Bank. They showed up at all the finest places, so his calculations must have worked.

It was fifteen minutes into a two-hour ordeal when Kate and Betty arrived, fashionably late. The twenty-five or so women there were chatting, drinking tea, as well as other beverages with a vintage. Sally, the Hadley maid, walked amongst the guests with trays of hors d'oeuvres. When she came alongside her employers, she would give them a wry smile. They had offered her a full day's salary in addition to whatever the Miltons would pay.

Betty sidled up to Kate after about twenty minutes. "Are you getting any hints of maids missing?"

"Not a word."

Evelyn Milton took a wine glass and tapped it with a spoon. "Ladies, ladies!" she raised her voice. "Attention, please." The women began to gather around her.

"Betty, don't you think that she looks like a stuffed white sausage with that dress?" Kate whispered. Betty coughed hard several times, trying not to laugh.

"Ladies, I would like to introduce my son, Charles Gardner!" A young man in his early 20's stepped forward. He was tall, handsome and well-poised. He was dressed in a very continental way, all white, with a navy blue sports jacket. He had no tie, but sported a cravat, instead. Smiling, young Charles saluted the ladies, with a slight bow.

"He recently graduated from Oxford," the proud mother announced. The ladies clapped politely. "And, after the Season, he will be joining his step-father at the Federal Reserve Bank." The ladies clapped again.

Kate leaned to Betty's ear. "When does she put out the ad for a wife for her son?" Betty shook with silent laughter, trying hard not to spill her tea.

Evidently, some of the other women had the same idea. They crowded around the young man to shake hands and make small talk. The sisters stood in the line for ten minutes before they got up to Charles.

Betty took his hand and introduced herself. "I am Elizabeth Hadley. My sister, Katherine, and I live next door. If there is anything we can do for you, do not hesitate to ask. As a matter of fact, your mother had to borrow our maid, tonight, since Mary

appears to be missing."

Charles faces blanched then he looked away for a moment before looking back. Kate noticed it.

"I could use a lady to show me around. I have been away for four years, you see," he said, grinning. He continued to hold her hand, and put his left hand over it.

"Sorry," Betty stepped back from the young man, almost stepping on Kate's toes, pulling her hand away at the same time. "I'm taken," she fibbed.

"Same with me," Kate added from behind Betty's shoulder. "But we will tell our friends you are looking." Betty nodded in agreement as they turned away. The two walked towards the buffet table to place their cups down. "I have had enough," Betty added. "Are you ready to go?"

"Yes, I am talked out. Let us say goodbye to Evelyn." Kate responded.

They caught Evelyn between people to talk to, and told her they had to leave.

"Oh, dearies! Thank you for coming. Did you get to meet Charles?" she ogled. "He is looking for companions for the evening, you know. I thought you two might be available until he finds someone more appropriate, errrr, younger."

"How long has he been back in the States, Evelyn?" Kate asked.

"It has only been two months. He has been studying his career options, and now that that is out of the way, he wants to look at his social options." She smiled broadly as she talked about her only son.

"We wish him all the luck in his future endeavors," Kate smiled. "Will you be going to Newport for the Season?"

"Oh, yes!" Evelyn gushed. "We leave in a week! George will drive down on weekends and Charles and I will enjoy the next two months, immensely!"

"So, if we do not see you before you leave, I wish you a lovely summer!" Betty offered. Then, in a low voice, she added, "Have you heard anything about Mary?"

"Not a word," Evelyn responded in an equally low voice. "I cannot, in all honesty, give Mary her job back when she returns."

Betty patted Evelyn's hand. "I do not blame you, my dear. However, we did promise Father that we would see him for an hour tonight, so we are going to leave a little early." The sisters kissed Evelyn and left to get their wraps.

Walking the few steps to their own house, Kate turned to her sister. "Do you see that young man as odd?"

"Well, he certainly is forward. But, then, his mother apparently is pushing his interests."

"Did you see, when you mentioned Mary's name this evening, that his face changed, for just a moment?"

"I did notice that but I thought perhaps he was angry that she took off and ruined his mother's plans."

"I think you are wrong, here. I think, when a person looks away in the middle of a conversation, like that, he is hiding something."

"Kate, I think you need to study under a psychologist. But, perhaps Father can lend some comments. We will ask at dinner."

TUESDAY EVENING

Dinner was a formal occasion at the Hadleys'. Dr. Hadley, professor of psychiatry at Harvard Medical School, returned to his house every evening at 5. Dinner was promptly at 6:30. Betty and Kate were mandated to explain their own missing maid, and why James was serving. Luckily, Cook knew how much Dr. Hadley hated change. So, she made his favorite, lamb chops with apple jelly. It helped somewhat.

After dinner, the three Hadleys retired to his study to discuss the missing maid problem over brandy.

"So, ladies, you have a missing girl, a despondent boyfriend, a fight between two unknown men and a charming, albeit too flirtatious young man who hasn't been home in four years."

"Do not forget the vandalized swan boat, Father."

"Ah, yes, I did. Did I read something about that in the Evening Globe?" Dr. Hadley put down his snifter, got up from his chair and went to his desk. He picked up the newspaper, brought it back to his chair and adjusted his gooseneck floor lamp. Holding up the newspaper, he flipped through the pages until he found what he was looking for.

Elizabeth A Martina

"Ah, here it is. 'A swan boat was found vandalized at the Gardens' pond this morning. The manager discovered the vandalism when unlocking the boats just before 9am. The boat in question had one bench out of the three broken, with one leg missing. The leg appears to have been broken off with a hammer. So far, the metal leg has not been found, despite a search throughout the pond area.'"

"That is pretty much what the police officer told us," Kate

noted.

"Are you two sure that this has anything to do with the maid?" Hadley asked, refolding the newspaper.

"Only that Tony Greco was mourning about the swan boats. It is just too much of a coincidence."

"Did you believe him when he said that he allowed Mary to go home alone?"

"I think we did until we talked to the concession stand fellow, who talked about the fight he heard." Dr. Hadley shook his head in disbelief at the events his daughters got themselves into.

"So, Father, we want to know what ways there are of telling if a person is lying just by watching his facial expressions."

"My dear, there are many ways." Hadley sat up straighter in his chair and adjusted his tie as if he

35

was about to begin a lecture at the medical school. "For example, a man who is lying will tend to look away for an instant before answering a question." Betty nudged Kate's arm. "However, there are also verbal hesitations, for example, hemming and hawing while speaking. Or over-exaggerated hand motions."

"Tony was getting dressed as we spoke to him," Kate mentioned.

Hadley raised his eyebrows and looked at his daughters questioningly.

"Oh, Father! Don't worry. He had on his pants and undershirt. He just was putting on a dress shirt and belt," Kate explained. "He just wouldn't look at us, much. He was concentrating on his dressing."

"That means he was uncomfortable dealing with the subject matter, not that he was either lying or guilty."

"What about Charles Gardner?" Betty asked, leaning forward towards her father.

"Eye movement is not well established as a sign of lying. It can mean that Charles was thinking about Mary when you mentioned her name."

"A Boston Brahmin even knowing the name of a maid is fairly unusual, Father," Betty commented.

"Perhaps he knew her enough to speak to her?"

"Father! A young man who has been at Oxford for four years comes home to Boston and, within two months, in a new home, he is speaking to a little maid from Ireland. Enough to remember her name?"

Hadley looked at his girls, realizing that they had been well protected from the world, even yet, at 22 and 23 years of age. "You do not realize how many rich people have ruined poor little maids in a short period of time."

"Oh, Father, you have been reading too many cheap novels!" Betty exclaimed.

"Mark my word, my dears. If our neighbor is involved, the disappearance could be nasty. But, you have little proof, and I think that you will discover that you have blown this all out of proportion. Watch yourselves. And, Kate, your young man is a police detective. Hasn't he warned you, yet."

Kate looked wide-eyed at her father at the mention of Casey. She smiled, slightly. "Yes, he has already warned us," she said quietly.

"Listen to him, my dear," Dr. Hadley said as he stood up. "Use your common sense, ladies." The hall clock began to strike the hour. He looked out the windows, the sun was setting and most of the light was now from the street poles. "It is my reading time. I am going to sit with a good book for a while."

Armed with some pointers, the two sisters kissed him good night and left for their own rooms. It was 9:00pm. Kate had just gotten comfortable on her chaise lounge when Casey called her, around 9:30, for their nightly chat.

"Evelyn Milton's son, Charles, is quite spoiled, I would say," Kate began after hearing about Casey's day.

"How can you say that with only an hour of acquaintance?" Casey's irritated voice responded. He had had a busy day.

"He presumes that Betty and I are available to him," Kate pouted, looking for a sympathetic ear.

"Ah, then. He is rich, educated and good-looking, I assume," Casey chided.

"He is all those things, but not as good-looking as you," Kate responded, flirtatiously. "And hardly as mature."

"So, exactly what did he say to you?" Casey asked warming to the subject.

"He said, 'I could use a lady to show me around.'"

"Immature, yes. But it hardly proves he is spoiled."

"His step-father got him a job at the Federal

Reserve," Kate tried to make her point. "But he is not going to start until after the summer Season is over."

"Kate," Casey sounded impatient. "You have lived among the Brahmins all your life. You know that is not unusual. What is your real problem with this kid?"

Kate sighed and switched the receiver to the other ear. "You are right, Casey. There is just something about him that makes me feel creepy. I can't put my finger on it."

"I think this mysterious disappearance of the maid is getting you all tied up in knots. I suggest a hot cup of tea and some light reading and call it an early night." Casey sounded like he needed an early night.

"I suppose you are right, Casey," Kate replied, looking at the pile of new books she had not arranged on her bookcase yet.

"Tell you what!" Casey brightened up for a moment. "That new movie about the Civil War that you have been talking about is playing all over. Maybe we can go see it this weekend."

"That would be lovely! It will get my mind off of missing persons."

"I will find out the times and tell you tomorrow

night. Good, night, Kate!"

Kate hung up and turned towards her pile of books. Changing her outlook, she went through her newest acquisitions and pulled out *Gone With the Wind*. Taking it over to her chaise, she switched on the light and curled up to read, pulling out the ribbon marking the place where she had left off. After an hour, she went to bed. Her last thoughts were that she had never heard Sally return.

WEDNESDAY MORNING

At breakfast the next morning, Sally looked droopy. The food was set out fine, but the table was set wrong, cup handles were turned around and the knives and spoons were reversed. Dr. Hadley, not a stickler on etiquette, did not notice. He had his coffee and eggs and had left by the time the sisters appeared at 8:30. They, on the other hand, noticed immediately.

"Sally, you look like you did not sleep well. Are you all right?" Betty asked as soon as she sat. James was there to pour her coffee as soon as she picked up her napkin.

"Do you need the afternoon off?" added Kate.

Sally was scowling, completely out of character. She had worked for the Hadleys for three years. She was well-trained and knew enough not to be hostile or testy. However, Sally was comfortable enough with the two young ladies to confide in them when necessary.

"James, would you leave us for ten minutes?" Kate saw this breakfast as one of those necessary times.

When James left and closed the door, Sally blurted

out, "I will never work for Mrs. Milton again. Even if you fire me."

Betty put down her coffee cup hard, the sweet brown liquid splashing over the rim. "What happened, Sally?"

"Mrs. Milton cannot make up her mind what she wants. Then she argues." The sisters laughed until they saw her still-troubled face, and stopped. They watched her go through some moments of debate. Sally's hands rolled into fists. "And the son! I am not one to speak ill of my betters, but he is a boor!" Her voice rose and her chin trembled.

Betty pulled out the chair beside her. "Sally, I want you to sit down and pull yourself together. Take a deep breath. Then explain yourself." Sally sat, looking out of place, watching the faces of her two employers.

She took a deep breath and began. "Not only was he asking for young ladies, he wanted to MEET with ME! Last night, I had to fight him off."

The two sisters both gasped. It was known that many rich men used maids, but Betty and Kate were modern. They had an enlightened view of the poor and rich.

"Oh, Sally, dear, I am so sorry!" Kate interjected. "Are you quite well?"

"I gave him a black eye!" Sally suddenly grinned. With that, the sisters laughed so hard that James returned to see to the ruckus.

"Miss Hadley, is everything quite right?" His look of concern changed to a grin when he heard the explanation. He nodded. "I have heard about this young man. He is not one to take no for an answer," he added as he took the empty coffee carafe back to be refilled.

"You are not going to fire me, are you?" Sally asked anxiously.

"No. Of course not," Betty assured her. "It sounds like he got what he deserved."

"Perhaps Mary had to run away to get away from him?" Kate speculated, looking at Betty.

Betty looked seriously at Sally. "If she has run away, we must find her friends and ask some questions."

"I think we should start out with Tony Greco. He would know if she left. He may have been stalling for time, when we questioned him yesterday. Maybe giving her time to get far

enough away. That would account for his being so upset."

"But first," Betty said. "Let's eat. I am hungry."

43

Sally smiled. "I feel like I am involved with your detecting work." She got up and grabbed some dishes from the buffet, placing them on the table.

James handed the ladies the Morning Post, refolded almost exactly as it had come to the house. Dr. Hadley had already read it. The sisters split the sections.

Fifteen minutes into quiet reading and eating, Kate let out a squeak. Betty's head popped up. "What was that?"

Kate lowered the paper to look at her sister. "Listen to this! 'Police found a body last night in the basement of a house in the North End. They report that the body belongs to a young female, probably 16 to 18 years of age, blond, with long braids. There were no identifying marks or papers on the body. Since she was blonde, police are assuming she is not Italian and suspect foul play.' Doesn't that sound like Mary?!"

Betty looked across the table in shock. "The body was found in the North End? Where Tony lives?" She gulped hard and stared.

Kate looked at her watch. 'Casey should be at work soon. Hasn't the precinct at the North End informed the Sudbury St. precinct yet?" She threw down the paper and got up from the table, leaving her breakfast little touched. "Sally, please apologize to

Cook for me. But this is too important for breakfast!" Kate knew Cook was insulted when her meals were not consumed.

She walked to the door. "Betty, are you coming?"

Betty dotted her lips with her napkin and rose from her chair. "Sally," she directed herself to the maid for a moment. "When we get back, I want to talk to you. But I think we have the answer to Mary's disappearance. Tony!" She left the room and ran upstairs for her hat and purse while Kate rang for the car.

On the way to the Sudbury Street station, Betty and Kate discussed this new information and their role.

"Kate. did Casey file the missing person's report on Mary?" Betty asked as she negotiated the morning traffic.

"I am not sure. He got involved with the vandalism case and was at work until almost 8. I was so tired, I forgot to ask."

"If he did not file, then that explains why the North End police didn't identify the body, assuming it is Mary. But, even if he did file, they may not have gotten all the reports by 2am or whenever the Post went to print."

Betty pulled to the curb on Sudbury and they got out, resetting their hats and grabbing their purses.

They ran up the front stairs and through the glass front doors.

"Hello, Sgt Ryan." Kate greeted, coming to a full stop before the main desk.

"Two days in a row? Are you girls getting advice on your latest hijinks?" The heavy-set sergeant grinned.

Kate grinned back and blew him a kiss, then waltzed away, followed by Betty. Their heels clicking on the linoleum floors once again turned heads, but they were too much on a mission to notice.

Luckily, Lt. Roach was alone in his office. Kate knocked on the open door and entered before he could look up from his work. The face he displayed was worn and drawn.

"Oh, Casey! Are you all right?" Kate's concerned voice made him smile, slightly.

He stood and walked around the desk. He gave Kate a big hug.

"I am so sorry, Kate. I didn't give your missing person enough credence."

Kate pulled back. "So, the dead body really is Mary?"

"She is still a Jane Doe, until we can get a positive

identification. Does she have family here?"

"I don't think so. I heard she came over from Ireland last year."

"Well, then, would either of you be able to identify the body?"

The girls looked at each other, then back at Casey and both nodded.

"Then would you mind coming over to Mass General and identifying her? Assuming it is Mary."

"I will," Kate piped up immediately." He picked up the phone and called the coroner's office, arranging a visit in the next half hour.

"Betty, are you coming?" Kate turned her attention to her sister.

"You go with Casey. I'll follow in the roadster. I need a few minutes to get prepared." She was the more upset of the two.

"Betty, are you all right? You look pale," Kate noted.

"I just haven't seen many dead bodies. I certainly did not expect Mary to be one!"

Kate extended her gloved hand and squeezed her sister's shoulder. "We are in this together," she said reassuringly.

Casey grabbed his hat off the rack and took Kate's elbow, guiding her out the door. Betty followed, a little slowly.

A mile west on Cambridge Street rose the impressive White Building of the Massachusetts General complex. Casey steered his way onto Allen Street and found curbside parking. Betty pulled in a minute later.

The medical examiner's office was in the basement of an older building. It took ten minutes of walking beneath heating ducts and bare lightbulbs to reach their destination.

"This place looks like a scary movie set." Kate whispered, sidling closely to Casey. He looked down at her and grimaced.

"Here we are," he pointed out a wooden door with a frosted glass window. Painted on the window in large letters was "Dr. Tracy B. Mallory". The three walked into an office. The secretary at the desk, a woman in her mid-40s, smiled, recognizing Casey.

"Good morning, Detective Roach. Are you here about the Jane Doe?"

"Yes, thank you, Miss Pierce. I have someone who may be able to identify the body."

"That would be fine," she responded in her crisp voice. "Have a seat and I will notify a clerk." She spoke briefly on the intercom while they sat in the hard, worn leather seated chairs.

A middle-aged man in a long white clinic coat came in after 5 minutes. "Detective Roach! Welcome back!"

Casey grimaced. "Thanks, Jack!"

"So, we have a witness who can identify the Jane Doe?"

"Actually, two. If she is who we think she is."

Jack turned to the sisters. "Are you ladies ready?" Silently the two stood and followed him and Casey, through a door and down a poorly lit corridor to another door marked "Morgue". Kate and Betty each took a deep breath and followed the men inside.

In the middle of the floor were two gurneys. The bodies, covered with white sheets, were hidden, except for the feet. It was obvious that one was a male and one a female. Jack walked over to the female and crooked his finger to encourage the girls to come closer.

As they approached very gingerly, Jack chuckled. "Are you ready?" he asked.

They gulped and nodded. He pulled back the sheet to show the corpse's head and bare shoulders.

Betty's hand flew to her mouth and her eyes welled up. Kate backed up half a step and bit her lower lip.

Casey put his hand on Kate's shoulder. "It's Mary, isn't it?" Kate looked at the pale face, the closed eyes, the messy braids. As a neighbor, Kate had seen the Martins' maid enough times to recognize her. She turned away.

Casey took the sisters out for coffee afterwards. The little diner at Scollay Square was an enchanting place with excellent coffee and pastries. After a cup, Kate and Betty could think more clearly.

"So, it is no longer a missing person's inquiry. It is a murder investigation." Casey tried to break the quiet. "So, who do we have as a possible perpetrator?"

"Tony?" Kate suggested. "She was found only a block from his place."

"Charles Gardner," Betty added. "She worked right there at his home."

"We always investigate known subjects of interest first," Casey began. "I am going over to the police station on Causeway after we are done here. I want to take a look at the photos and the area around the scene. I need to figure out if she was killed there or dumped there."

"We can go question Tony Greco for you," Kate offered.

"Oh, no, you don't!" Casey's eyes bored into the two of them. "This is now a matter for the Boston police. I do not want you two sneaking around."

"Then we can talk to the Miltons?"

"No!"

"Then what can we do?" Kate pouted.

"Go play cards. Go to a movie. Just don't get involved with my work." Casey's face was getting red. The girls sighed.

"Look, ladies, I have got to get back to work." Casey stood up and leaned over to kiss Kate's forehead. "I will call you tonight," he promised.

Betty sat back and crossed her arms, watching him leave. "I am not going to sit around waiting for him to solve this crime," she pouted. "I am going to ask some of the maids in the neighborhood if they know anything."

"Wait!" Kate's eyes opened wide. "The Miltons' cook! If Mary had any concerns, she might have confided in her!"

"That's an idea! Can we get our cook, or, maybe Sally, to ask questions?" Betty brightened up.

"No. Sally won't go there and Cook is busy. Let us go right now, before Evelyn gives her cook another party to prepare for," Kate added sarcastically.

The sisters put a quarter on the table for a tip and walked out to the busy square. It was only a matter of minutes before they came to a halt in front of their house. They walked next door and around to the back, delivery entrance. Betty rang the bell and played nervously with her gloves.

The cook answered the door. Her eyes glistened with perpetual happiness, but the wrinkle between her eyebrows showed concern. She looked puzzled at the two well-dressed sisters standing at a door reserved for delivery men.

"Miss Hadley? And Miss Hadley!" She looked from one to the other. "What is the meaning of coming to this door?" She opened the door wider to let them in.

"We want to talk with you, Mrs. Kelly!" Kate piped up.

Cook looked at their faces and knew before they could say anything. "It is about Mary. I know." She ushered them into her private sitting room, off the servants' dining room. "Sit in here and I will bring tea." The sisters sat together on an upholstered loveseat. The cook quickly returned with a tray and placed it on the small table in front of the sisters.

She poured and handed out cups to the two. Then she sat in her wooden rocker.

"Now, then, dearies. Tell me what you know."

Kate smiled slightly. "Have you seen the morning paper?"

"Not personally. But I heard the rumor. Do you think it is Mary?"

"Oh, Mrs. Kelly," Betty's lower lip trembled. "We went to the morgue. We saw the body. It is Mary."

The cook put her cup down on the end table and looked at them sternly. "What were you doing in the morgue?"

"I am seeing a young man who is a police detective. He had been looking into this as a missing person's report. Then, this morning…." Kate shrugged. "He asked us to go look."

The older woman paled obviously. "Was she…hurt?"

"We saw no marks on her face and shoulders."

"Is there a cause of death?"

"Not yet. Maybe tomorrow we will hear."

The poor woman teared up a little and slowly shook her head. "The poor child. She was so lonely."

Betty asked. "I know she came over from Ireland last year. But was there any family here?"

The woman shook her head. "She has been with us almost six months. She didn't say much about them."

"Was she dating?" Kate asked.

Mrs. Kelly sat and looked out the window for a moment. "Well, there was that nice Italian boy who drives for some family over on Arlington. But there was something else going on."

The sisters both anxiously leaned forward.

Still looking out the window, Mrs. Kelly continued. "She would get moody or anxious, but not in any pattern related to that boy. So, I think she may have had several boys she was seeing. I didn't pry. After all, here I am an old lady in my 50s. She is still a child. I wouldn't get involved in a child's head games. No. No." She shook her head again.

Betty started looking in her purse for a pen and paper. "What kind of behavior was Mary showing earlier this week?"

Cook paused for a moment. "She was very moody, quick to whine and complain to me. But, not to Mrs. Milton, of course."

Kate and Betty looked at each other, reading each

other's thoughts. "How long has she been acting this way, being moody some days and fine others?"

"Oh, a few months, I guess. I was just getting to like her, like a niece, you know." Her voice caught and she took a handkerchief out of her pocket and dabbed at her eyes.

Betty made some notes. Then she stood. "I do not want you to get in trouble being away from the kitchen so long." She pulled on Kate's jacket shoulder. "We have to leave. I have several appointments this afternoon." She stepped to the door before Cook stood up. "Thank you for the tea."

Kate stood and walked to the door. Mrs. Kelly reached out and touched her hand. "You will let me know what you hear?"

"Oh, certainly."

"Don't mention tea or coffee to me until tomorrow," Kate insisted as the two walked back from the Miltons'. "So, we got some interesting comments from Mrs. Kelly. I am considering causes for all the emotional upheaval with Mary." They skirted the low-lying stone wall that marked the property boundary.

"I can think of one or two causes, myself. Let's see what Sally and Cook can get for us for a late lunch."

Betty looked at her watch. "It is already past 1:00. We can go over our suspicions while we eat."

They walked in the front door of the house to meet the grim visage of James on the hall phone.

"Ah, sir! They have just walked in." James put his hand over the mouthpiece and looked at Kate. "It is Lt. Roach. Are you available?"

Kate quickly reached for the receiver and James disappeared towards the kitchen. "Casey? Is everything all right?"

"The medical examiner's office just called. They completed the autopsy."

"How did she die?"

"Apparently, she was hit with something hard, long and cylindrical. She died several hours later. Internal bleeding. But that is not the surprising news."

"What do you mean?"

"She was pregnant. About 6 weeks along." Casey sighed. "That points to Tony, doesn't it?"

Kate was stunned and could not think of anything to say for a moment. "Well, yes and no. She was… I don't think standing in the foyer of my house is the best place to have this conversation. Can Betty and I come down this afternoon?"

"Sure. How about 3:00?"

"Yes. I have a few things to do first. That is perfect." They said their good-byes and Kate hung up, looking at Betty with a rather triumphant expression.

Betty was fixing her curly blonde hair before the mirror during the phone conversation and she had heard all of Kate's side. "You just put two and two together, didn't you?" she observed.

"I am thinking we have to look at Tony. She was with child, as they say."

Betty's eyebrows almost reached her hairline. "Exactly what I was surmising since Mrs. Kelly told us about Mary's emotions. And I wanted to see Tony as an innocent bystander. So much for my analysis of character."

Sally came into the foyer and heard the last two sentences. "Lunch is available, Miss Betty. And I have been snooping around asking questions for you. I have a few things to tell you."

In the breakfast room, a relaxed environment, unlike the formal

dining room, the Hadley sisters insisted that Sally sit with them, even if she was not going to eat. The sisters opted for some chicken soup and a cold chicken salad, which was available almost immediately.

"Tell us who you talked to and what they said," Betty eagerly insisted.

"You remember when you went to the Bridges' place yesterday morning?" Sally began. "Well, apparently, Mrs. Bridges was not at all happy that you came over and asked questions. She was heard yelling about it to her husband later. And one of the maids knows, knew, Mary." Here she winced a little for stumbling over the verb. "Well, that is Joan. And Joan and I are friends. Joan and Mary weren't exactly companions, but they talked."

Betty and Kate watched her as they ate and did not stop to encourage her. Sally continued. "It looks like Joan introduced Mary to Tony. About a month ago. He had only been working at the Bridges a little while. He was so handsome and suave. And Mary was so lonely all the time. Joan thought it would work out."

"We spoke to Tony. His accent was not bad. Why did Mr. Bridges complain about understanding him?'

"That was a big lie, begging your pardon for saying something bad about my betters, Miss Betty. Mr. Bridges just doesn't like guineas, Italians. He says they are dirty. No matter how many baths, they still look dark. So, they made the excuse that his accent was the problem. Mr. Bridges told his wife that she may not hire anyone else without his say-so."

Betty winced at those harsh words. "But does that have anything to do with Mary's going missing?"

"Joan said that she caught Tony and Mary in a compromising

situation two weeks ago. Maybe that is another reason why Tony got fired."

"Wait. Let's go back to what you said a minute ago. So, Tony and Mary met only a month ago?" Kate asked. Sally nodded.

Kate laid down her spoon and took a deep breath. "That puts a different spin on the story."

Sally looked at her quizzically. "What do you mean?"

"She was pregnant. Six weeks."

Sally's jaw dropped. "Well, if that's the case, it couldn't be Tony who is the father." She closed her eyes for a moment. Opening her eyes, she said, quietly, "Was Mary a run-around, do you think?"

"Have you heard of her with others?"

"No. But I am not much of a gossip, going after such information." Sally looked down at her hands. "I wish I had the answer."

Kate dabbed at her lips and pushed the empty plate away from her. "It would be helpful if you could talk to one or two more maids who knew Mary. If you would…"

Sally looked up. "I will. Thank you for letting me help you. It is truly exciting, but sad."

Kate stood up as Betty finished her last bite of lunch. "We have an appointment downtown at 3," she explained to Sally. "It isn't like Lt. Roach to want to talk about a case. Something else must have come up." She shrugged her shoulders. "Betty, dear, I am going to freshen up. I shan't be more than a minute." With that, Kate excused herself.

Back in Lt. Casey Roach's office at exactly 3:00, the sisters were sitting across the desk from an angry young man. Casey had the typewritten medical examiner's report in front of him. It was only one page, with two accompanying photos. Only the basics had been done. The whole report had been done in an hour.

"I am not angry at the medical examiner. I am angry that this is the state of investigation at this point in time." He sighed. "Here's what we know: Mary was pregnant, about six weeks or so. She had mud on her shoes. It is obvious that she fell, since on her right side, her leg and dress were also covered in mud. She had a huge black and blue mark on her left side, below the rib cage. She bled internally. Time of death was a little after midnight."

"That's it?"

"That is it."

"The fellow selling hotdogs said that the fighting and the screams came just before he was closing up, about 8:00. If that was Mary doing the screaming, what was she doing the last four hours of her life?"

"First of all, screams do not mean Mary was screaming. Second, the screams were at the Boston Gardens and she was found in the North End. Third, if it was Mary screaming at 8:00, she spent the last four hours suffering in agony."

Kate and Betty both recoiled on hearing Casey's synopsis. Kate looked at him in horror.

"Also, I received another piece of information in the past hour. The lawn mowers at the Gardens found something early this morning and it got turned over to us a few hours later." Casey opened a desk drawer and pulled out a cylindrical package of brown wrapping paper. He laid it on his desk and opened it. It was a foot and a half long red-painted tube, obviously broken on both ends, with a dark stain on one side. "Ladies, may I present what I think was the murder weapon. The broken leg of a swan boat bench."

Kate and Betty both got up to see it closer. "What is the stain?" Betty asked. "Rust?"

"Blood." Was Casey's terse reply. "It may be human." Both girls backed away in horror.

"Where did they find this?" Kate asked, a little shaken at the prospect that someone could die from this piece.

"It was in some undergrowth, on the other side of the Gardens from the pond. One of the attendants was doing some raking."

"Now, what happens?"

"We still don't know who, when, why or where this happened. I am guessing that if that pipe was the cause, then it probably happened there in the Gardens, somewhere and then got tossed. But why would she end up in the North End?"

"Because her boyfriend, of sorts, lived there. And it could get pinned on him?" Betty answered immediately.

"So, you are saying that the boyfriend could not have done it?" Casey asked cautiously.

"Well, it turns out, he could not be the father. He and Mary only met a month ago."

Casey's eyes grew wide. "This is not going to be an easy case, is it?" He leaned back in his chair. "Just because he was not the father, does not mean he didn't kill her. We need to question him. What else do you have that I don't know about?"

"Tony got fired a week ago. But not because of his accent. Because of his being Italian. And, a maid found him and Mary in a compromising situation. This might have added to the decision to fire him." Kate looked him in the eye to see if Casey believed her.

"And…," Betty broke in. "That Gardner man living next door to us. He is not out of the question. I think you should interview him."

"We are going over there this evening. I just wanted to see if you girls had any fresh information before I did."

"You told us to mind our own business."

"And I doubted you would. Look at all the information you brought me this afternoon."

The two smiled sheepishly.

"Can we go with you when you question Charles Gardner?"

"Of course not."

"But if we accidentally hear some of the interview, it won't be so bad, right?" Kate asked. He just looked at her and shook his head slowly.

WEDNESDAY EVENING

At 6pm, a black Boston City Police vehicle pulled up to the curb at Evelyn Milton's home. Casey got out and went to the front door which Harold, the butler, opened before Casey got close enough to knock.

"I am Lt. Roach from the Sudbury St. Precinct. I have an appointment to speak to Mr. Gardner."

The older butler hesitated, then moved aside to let Casey and his associate, Sgt. Perkins, into the house. "This way, gentlemen," Harold lead them into a small, front room. He indicated two very posh chairs "Please have a seat. I will tell Mr. Gardner that you have arrived."

The men stepped into the uncomfortably feminine receiving room. The chairs were curved, upholstered in pinks and oranges; the fake Duncan Phyfe couch was a vertically striped item. The depressively heavy curtains were opened only a few inches and the outside view was covered with an ivory chiffon. The men were not willing to sit down.

Evelyn Milton waltzed in, wearing an item that matched the sheer curtains. "How may I help you gentlemen?" she oozed, extending her hand. Casey shook her hand. Perkins imitated his boss.

"We were expecting to meet with Charles Gardner," Casey responded.

"My boy is so busy, getting ready for the Season. I am sure you understand. I sent him down to Newport for the day to suggest some renovations to our summer house."

"We had an appointment for 6:00 pm," Casey insisted.

"I am sure you can make it another time, my dear lieutenant. After all, the Season is only two weeks away and the contractors are only available now. You understand." She ended by fluttering her stubby eyelashes in an attempt to be flirtatious.

Casey was not willing to accept this poor regard for his profession. "Mrs. Milton, if your son is trying to evade my questioning, I can have him brought into my office at my convenience, in handcuffs."

The little woman put her hand on her ample chest and gulped in air. She quickly regained her composure and replied, "I will have you know that my husband is the president of the Federal Reserve Bank and will not accept any threats on his family."

Casey's face turned red. "And I will have you know that I am a lieutenant in the Boston detective squad and can arrest anyone who impedes my murder investigation." Casey bent down to reach her eye level and lowered his voice. "And that includes rich women."

Evelyn Milton could not come up with a single word, but simply looked at him in stupefaction. "How, how…dare you!" she managed to get out. Stepping to the bell pull, she summoned Harold, who must have been standing just the other side of the pocket doors. He opened and stepped in. "Get these two monsters out of my house!" she screamed at him. Harold was obviously used to her emotional outbursts. He simply nodded and stood aside for the men to precede him out of the room, away from the screaming that Mrs. Milton was keeping up.

As Harold opened the door for the two to leave, he looked at them apologetically. "I am sorry about the mix-up, gentlemen," he said, avoiding their eyes. The men tipped their hats and walked out the door.

As they approached the police car, Betty and Kate came around

from the back of the Milton house. Casey crooked an eyebrow and looked at them accusingly. "What are you up to, now?"

"We just stopped in to have late tea with the Miltons' cook, just before she was ready to serve appetizers," Kate said innocently.

"We can't help it if we heard the conversation through the thin walls," added Betty.

"It is not worth telling you to stop, isn't it," Casey said shaking his head. "Is your father home yet?" he asked, glancing over to the Hadley house.

"He will be, momentarily. Shall we go over to our yard to talk about what we found out?"

Casey sighed. "Perkins, move the car back away from the Miltons' house. Stay with the car while I find out what these two junior detectives have to say." Perkins got into the car.

Casey walked with his arm around Kate's shoulder and they went around the back to the patio.

Sitting on the patio was a wicker table and four matching chairs. There were glasses and a pitcher of lemonade. Sitting, Betty poured for each while Kate explained.

"Mrs. Kelly said that there was an argument earlier this afternoon between Gardner and Mrs. Milton. She sent him away with no uncertainty. She told him to come back tomorrow evening and to not wreck the car. Mrs. Kelly also said that she doesn't see what renovations could be done, since the place was all redecorated last spring."

Casey was taking a sip from his glass. His eyebrows rose over the rim. He put his glass down hard. "So, she lied to me. I wonder what was her motivation."

"Doesn't this make Gardner look guilty?" Betty

asked.

"It certainly does," Casey answered, squinting in thought. "But hardly conclusive."

"What are you thinking?" Kate looked at him concerned.

"I am trying to piece this together. With little success." Casey pushed back his chair. "I think I am going to go find this Tony Greco. He has to know more." He bent over and kissed Kate. "I will try to call you tonight. If not, don't worry."

Kate smiled up at him. "Good luck!" She watched him walk back to the car. Then she turned to Betty.

"Would you like a lovely ride in the country in the morning? Newport isn't more than three hours away."

"Oh, I would love to do that drive. And, maybe we can find why little Charlie went off!" The sisters heard their father come in through the open French doors. It was time to get ready for dinner.

THURSDAY MORNING

As soon as Dr. Hadley left for the university at 8:30, the sisters got off the breakfast table, finished dressing and took off on their trip. It was just before noon when they pulled up in front of the Milton summer home in Newport. Imposing, with a large circular driveway, the house looked newly painted. The landscaping was fresh and the gardens colorful. The bright blue SS Jaguar 100 that had been seen around Beacon Hill the past few months was parked in the driveway, right in front of the door.

"Well, he is here," Betty commented, sitting at the opposite curb, the engine purring. "What do we do now?"

"I think that we should go talk to him," Kate announced. She went to open the door when Betty put her gloved hand on Kate's arm.

"Wait! He is coming around the side of the house!" Kate turned to look. They watched Charles Gardner, all in white, walk over to his car and get in.

"Betty, how good are you at following people without getting caught?"

"Watch me," was the answer as the roadster pulled out into light traffic. They kept two cars between themselves and Gardner as often as possible and wound round the curved roads that followed the shoreline. Finally, the Jaguar pulled into the golf course and parked in the members only parking lot. Betty and Kate parked further out. Dr. Hadley was not a golfer and had no reason to join a club in the next state over.

The girls tried to follow him, but everyone had on white and

they lost him in the crowd. Unsure as to the next step, the girls decided to have lunch and regroup.

"I am sorry, ladies, but this restaurant is only open to members and their families," the hostess insisted. "I am sure that you will be able to find something satisfactory in town." She turned away.

"This is not what I wanted this afternoon," Betty complained. The two turned away, heads down in anger and embarrassment and ran right into a man dressed in white.

"Well, well, what have we here!" Charles Gardner was broadly smiling at the two, his black eye still well in evidence. "I was wondering who I would have lunch with and here are my two next door neighbors from Boston!" He grabbed a sister with each arm and marched up to the hostess. "Table for three." She directed them to a small table, slightly isolated in a bay window, handed them menus and left.

"All right, ladies," Charles' smile was gone. "What are you doing here?"

Betty stumbled over her words, trying to make sense of their escapade. "We wanted to ask you some questions. That's all."

"Like that police officer last night?"

"He is a detective, not an officer," Kate interrupted.

"Well, I don't have anything to tell him about Mary," Charles insisted, keeping his eyes on the menu.

"Yes, you do, Charles Gardner," Betty hissed. "Did you know that she was pregnant?"

Gritting his teeth, he put his menu down. "Are we having lunch or an interrogation?" His jaw jutted out making him look very determined. The sisters looked at each other and shrugged slightly.

"If we have a pleasant lunch with you, will you then answer our questions?" Betty was not sure she was doing the right thing.

"I will answer the questions that I want to. And, of course, since you have nothing over me, I have no obligation to answer any." Charles picked up his menu again and got absorbed in his lunch choices. The sisters tried to find something themselves.

After an extravagant luncheon of oysters and lobster

bisque, Charles signed his bill and leaned back in his chair. "I do not know what you want to ask, but I want it all done in private. I am not going to answer questions here." He glared at them. "I don't like being suspected of something I didn't do. Which is the only reason I am cooperating." He pushed his chair back and got up. "I am inviting you to my parents' place, away from others. I will speak to you for half an hour. And that is it." He started walking away and the sisters had to quickly grab their purses and gloves and chase after him.

The Mercedes Benz roadster had no difficulty keeping up with the Jaguar on the way back to the summer house. Betty parked behind Charles in the circular driveway and he led them up the steps to the front door. They entered into a cool foyer, done in blues and whites, with a nautical theme in the framed pictures and knick knacks. A maid came in from the back to check on the noise. Charles asked her for a pitcher of lemonade and some glasses. Then he escorted the ladies out to the patio overlooking the water.

The three settled into wicker chairs with deep blue gingham cushions. Kate kicked off her pumps for a few minutes, to cool off her feet. The day had become much warmer than expected.

Charles took a sip from his lemonade and put it down. He glanced at his watch. "You have half an hour," he pronounced.

"You know Mary is dead, correct?"

"I can read the papers. It was not hard to guess who the girl was that the police found in the North End."

"Did you know that she was pregnant?" Kate asked, not being subtle at all.

"I found out the night she died." Betty's eyebrows raised.

"Did she tell you or did someone else?" she asked.

"It was her day off. She came up the street at almost 7 when she was due back. I was just getting into my car and saw her. She did not look happy. So, I thought I would talk to her."

"Did you talk to her regularly?"

"Well, when I got home from England, Mother had recently hired her. I was homesick for England, truth be told. And she was homesick for Ireland. So, we kept each other company, you could say, one night. It was a bad idea and we never did it again."

"Humpf, taking advantage of a poor girl!" Betty gave him a disgusting look.

"Well, the next time I talked to her, except for professional talk, was the other night."

"And…?"

Charles sat back in his chair, put his hands across

his middle and locked fingers. He took a deep breath and began. "She said she had to talk to me. She said she needed money. And that she was pregnant. She said it was mine. We had a bit of a row there on the street. So, I said let's go down to the Gardens. We walked down the hill and she started crying. She said she had a boyfriend and that she asked him to marry her and give the baby a name. He said he didn't have money and could not do that. I said I would try to get my hands on some of my trust money if she would go away and never let the child know who his real father was. She was ready to agree when out of nowhere this tall, skinny guinea shows up and starts yelling at me."

"Excuse me, but where were you at that point?" Kate asked.

"Near the swan boats, but that doesn't matter. There are no witnesses. They had already closed for the night." Charles scowled at her. Betty and Kate exchanges looks.

"So, go on."

"He got in my face, accused me of rape and a bunch of other things. Gads! She is a maid, not a socialite! All this about nothing much!" Betty grabbed the arms of her chair to prevent herself from punching him.

"We started yelling back and forth. I threw a few

punches. He threw a few back. Mary was screaming, trying to make us stop. We got into quite a tussle and my jacket sleeve was ripped. The guinea walked off. Mary started crying and I said I would try to solve her problem as long as she kept her side of the bargain."

"As long as she didn't tell the child who his real father was?"

"Exactly. I figured a couple of thousand would shut her up. And she could probably make a go of it with this guinea or whoever."

"Is that how you left it?" Kate asked.

"Sure. I had a late date at the Cocoanut Grove. My jacket was a mess. I had to go change. The girl I was meeting was special. I wouldn't get another chance."

"So, Mary was alive when you left?"

"Sure, pretty little thing. She was teary, but certainly alive."

"Did you see her go back with Tony?"

"No. That guinea probably didn't have the guts to put up with something like that. He probably went home."

"So," Kate surmised. "You just let her walk around the Gardens by herself. At sunset."

"Like I said, I was busy. I had an important date."

"So, you went home, changed jackets and left?"

"Well, not exactly. I went in the house and Harold saw the jacket. I felt I had to tell him why. He has been with the family since I was a baby. In some ways he is like the wise uncle. As long as he doesn't let it get to his head and forget his place. You know what I mean?" Charles chuckled.

"What did he say when you told him?" Kate asked.

"He looked at me seriously and said, 'I will take care of it.' I don't know what he had in mind," Charles added and shrugged his shoulders. "I figured he would talk to her when she got home and tell her that she would be fired." He snorted. "Can't have pregnant maids, you know."

Betty's face blanched. "I think we have heard enough," she said, looking at Kate. She stood and looked at Charles. "I thank you for the luncheon and the lemonade. And the explanation." She took a deep breath. "If you are telling the truth, there will be no further reason to talk to us. And I do hope you are telling the truth." She stepped away from the chair and towards the door.

"You don't want my deep apologies for screwing the girl in the first place?" Charles smiled, still sitting.

Kate gave him a withering look. "I doubt you could." She stepped across his extended legs and walked off.

The girls were silent on the way home. Three hours of silence, punctuated by glances at a map to verify directions. Thinking about the circumstances just before Mary's death was uncomfortable at best. Finally, Kate broke the silence.

"Do you think that Evelyn Milton or the butler, Harold, had anything to do with this?"

"You have a good question. But who would risk a life sentence in jail when $5,000 could fix it?" Betty responded pensively. "I would rather spend the money."

Kate nodded in agreement. "I wonder what Casey found out from Tony. I hope he found him."

"We are almost home. You will know in half an hour," Betty noted as she negotiated the traffic in Framingham.

As soon as the sisters pulled up to the curb at the house, Kate ran in and picked up the receiver in the front hall while Betty went upstairs to freshen up for dinner. Kate dialed the police station and was connected with Casey in a minute.

"Hello, Casey! I was hoping to get you before you left!"

"I tried to call several times today. Where have you been?" Casey replied, anxiously. "I have a favor to ask."

"And I have information for you! What is the favor?"

"Do you have a nice evening dress you can wear tonight? We are going to the Cocoanut Grove for drinks after supper."

"Oh, Casey! How nice! What is the occasion?"

"We are going to talk to Tony. I found out he just got a job there as a busboy. He is never at his apartment. This is the best time to get him."

"Come pick us up at 8:30."

"Us?"

"Well, you can't expect Betty to sit on pins and needles all night waiting for me to get home!"

Casey laughed. "Of course not! Are you going to wait til then to tell me what you did all day?"

"I think I will. You can't yell at a girl in a chiffon gown," Kate teased and hung up immediately. She ran upstairs to Betty's room. Her sister was at her closet deciding what to wear for dinner.

"What do you have that would look good at a nightclub in three hours?"

Betty turned around holding two potential dresses and looked at her dumbfounded. "Where and why?"

"We are going to the Cocoanut Grove to question Tony. Apparently, Casey found out that Tony has a job there."

"That sounds like fun," Betty said dourly. "Did you tell Casey about today's little trip?" She turned around to replace the dresses and moved to her other closet, the one with the evening dresses.

"No. We will tell him tonight. Maybe we can all sort it out over the music." Kate chuckled and went to her room to find the right dress to wear for the night's events.

Dr. Hadley had his monthly dinner with his faculty and was just walking in the door when Kate walked down the stairs dressed for the evening. Her gown was a peach silk, the skirt cut on the bias so that it floated around her ankles. The backless top was covered by a matching chiffon jacket with ruffed sleeves. Her upswept dark curls contrasted well with the peach and Dr. Hadley stood in the foyer in stunned silence.

"You look like your mother," he muttered in wonder. Kate ran down the rest of the stairs and threw her arms around his neck, kissing him soundly.

"Thank you, Father. I thought she was so beautiful. That is the

nicest thing you could say to me!"

"So, where are we going tonight?" Dr. Hadley asked.

"To the Cocoanut Grove," Betty responded, walking down the same stairway. Dr. Hadley was again, impressed. Her pale blue gown, cut very much the same way, with a tight bolero top, showed off her blonde hair perfectly.

"My two bookends," Hadley smiled. "Shall we have a drink before you go?" The three linked arms and walked into his study.

"Who are you going with?" He winked as he poured gin into a shaker. "Pardon an old father from asking too many questions." In seconds, he handed them both a martini.

"Actually, Casey is working tonight and asked us along," Kate responded, sipping her drink.

"What kind of work does a detective do in a nightclub?" Hadley scowled.

"He has found a witness to the murder of the Miltons' maid. He works there. Maybe he can help us get to the truth."

"Us?" Hadley sat down hard in his chair.

"Well, Father, we got ourselves involved and now we just have to know what happened," Betty insisted. She grinned over the rim of the martini glass.

Dr. Hadley rolled his eyes. "Do I have to worry about you two, now?"

"I don't think so, Father," Kate leaned over and kissed his forehead. "It is just going to be a late snack and cocktails and Casey will try to find the young man. He will just talk." She patted his shoulder and set down her empty glass. She picked up her purse from the end table and stepped to the door.

"Good night, Father."

Betty, right behind her, blew him a kiss. "Don't wait up!"

Dr. Hadley, alone in his study with his martini, looked out the large front window and saw Casey Roach's five-year old green Opel Cabriolet sitting at the curb. The detective was in his tux, opening the door for the sisters to climb in. He walked around the car, looking very comfortable in the Beacon Hill world. Dr. Hadley silently gave the young man a salute with the last of his drink.

The Cocoanut Grove had been the place to be in

Boston, back in the late 20s. Then it nose-dived in popularity during the depths of the Depression. In the past year, it had climbed back into popularity. And crowds. The Opel found parking on Church St, two blocks from the club. The three could hear the loud orchestra playing before they got to the building.

The interior was packed, as it always was on Thursday, Friday and Saturday nights. The Tahitian décor was shimmering with moonlight: the roof opened for those who wished to dance under the stars. The twelve-piece orchestra had been playing since 8 and at 8:45 they took a break. The three were lucky; they could hear the maître d' explain the available seating.

Having been seated a comfortable distance from the dance floor, Casey remained relaxed while starting to scout the floor.

"Are you expecting Tony to show up?" Kate asked.

"He is working as a busboy, I am told. So, he should be out on the floor, somewhere." Casey sat bolt upright in his chair. "I found him. The only skinny Italian kid in the place." He cocked his head to the right and the girls followed his eyes. There was a cleaner looking man than the one they had met earlier in the week. It was obvious that he was new to his job. He was carrying the tray very awkwardly.

"That's the man," Betty acknowledged.

Casey called over the maître d', a man in his mid-forties, putting on a little weight but still looked good in a tuxedo. "You have a new young man working here. Name is Tony Greco."

"Certainly, Lieutenant. Just started yesterday. Do you have a problem with him?"

"No, Jonathan. I just wish to speak with him. When you see he has a few moments, could you please send him over?"

"Certainly, Lieutenant." He nodded and moved away to the next person signaling for him.

"Will Jonathan remember, do you think?" Kate asked. "He seems so busy."

"He'll remember, all right. This place is one step ahead of the police all the time. Jonathan manages to keep it legal most of the time." Betty and Kate had both heard stories, which surprised them every time.

The orchestra came back and started playing. Couples glided onto the dance floor. Kate and Casey were no different. Betty danced several sets with young men who found her irresistible.

The dinners were served at 9:00, lobsters and rice. The three kept to their drinks and hors d'oeuvres. At 9:45, the orchestra took a break, again, and some of the dinner group left. It was quiet for a few minutes and Jonathan, the maître d' came over with Tony Greco.

Tony was startled to recognize the Hadleys and took a step back. Jonathan grabbed hold of the young man's shirt. "If the lieutenant wants to speak with you, you speak to him." Tony took a step forward, thanks to a jab from the maître d'.

Casey pulled out the unused fourth chair. "Sit down, Mr. Greco. This shouldn't take too long."

Tony sat, hands clasped together, on the table. "I think I know what you want," he said, glancing sidelong at the sisters. "I read in the paper that she was dead. But, I swear to God, I did not do it." He reached up to his chest and started fingering the crucifix that was obviously hiding beneath his white shirt.

"Look, Mr. Greco," Casey began. "We are not here to accuse you of anything. We just really want to find out what happened that night." He waited for Tony to turn and look at him, which he did after looking at the sisters, appealingly.

Tony took a deep breath. His eyes welled up and spilled over. "She told me she was pregnant. That it was not mine." He looked at Casey and his voice cracked. "We only did it once!" He wiped a tear rolling down his cheek. "She said she loved me and wanted me to be the father of the baby." Tony covered his eyes with both hands, apparently in an attempt to blot out the vision of that moment. "Then she said she was going to talk to the father. Her boss's son. She thought the man should at least support the child."

"Did you go with her to the house?" Casey was writing down notes in his strange shorthand.

"No. She told me to go home and she would contact me in a day or two. She didn't have any more time off til Sunday."

Casey looked at him. "So, did you go home?"

"No. I was too worked up. I figured I would stay at the Gardens til dark. What was I gonna do? Go up to my dump and smoke cigarettes all night?"

"What happened next?" Kate broke in. Casey gave her a look of restraint.

"About half an hour later, she comes back with a blond WASP. They are all chummy. I snapped. I saw them walk around the place and I ran over to them and confronted him. I didn't know if he was gonna steal my girl! So…I threw the first punch. He's in good shape," Tony added, rubbing his right shoulder. "He beat me pretty good." His lower lip started to quiver. He had to take a deep breath to continue. "She started screaming and we were fighting. I tore his jacket. It was a nice one too, like yours, Lt. Roach." Tony reached out a finger to stroke the material on Casey's arm. "Real nice."

Betty and Kate watched Tony's face. They decided that he was telling the truth.

"After I tore his jacket, he just stopped. He said he wouldn't press charges. That he had to go. And he would think about Mary's request. He said it all while he was trying to clean himself up and look presentable. You know, brush his sleeves and tighten his tie. He gave Mary a dirty look, like it was all her fault. He took off and Mary just looked at me. She didn't say nothing. She took off after him."

"Did you go after her?" Casey asked.

"No. Her look was pretty bad. Like, for a minute she hated me. I figured I would stay out for a while and see if she would come back. I waited until the church bells rang 9 pm. Then I headed for the Park Street Station to catch the trolley home. I couldn't sleep or anything. And, before noon, these two," pointing to the sisters, "come knocking on my door." He leaned back in his chair and folded his arms. "That's all I got."

The orchestra was getting ready for the next set. Jonathan came over to the table. "Are you finished? He is needed on the floor."

Casey folded his notebook and put his pen in his

pocket. "We are all done here. Thank you for being honest with me, Mr. Greco." He extended his hand and Tony shook it in silence, then disappeared into the crowd and back to work.

Casey turned to the girls. "I am not sure he is telling the truth. Sounds too pat. Oh, woe is me, you know?"

Betty stopped him by putting her hand across the dishes and

touching him. "I think we can corroborate his story."

Casey looked from one girl to the other. "What did you do?" The music began. It began as a quiet piece, Rhapsody in Blue, the 15-minute version.

"Well," smiled Kate. "We just happened to go for a ride today. It was just so beautiful! And we just happened to run into Charles Gardner. We got to talking," she fluttered her eyes at him and ran her finger up his jacket sleeve. "And he told us a few things." She fluttered her eyes again.

"Wait a minute. Charles Gardner is out of town, at their summer home. In Newport. Rhode Island."

"Well… yes… we… heard." Kate said quietly, trying to smile at him.

"Did you go to Newport today, after I told you not to get involved?" Casey glared at her.

"You didn't tell us we couldn't go out to lunch. Or which restaurant to pick." Betty reminded him.

"You girls are going to get me fired some day!" Casey moaned, closing his eyes. He breathed deeply to calm himself. Finally opening his eyes, he glared at them. "And what did Mr. Gardner tell you?" He put his chin on his open hand and elbow on table, assuming a casual position.

"He told about the ripped jacket," Betty began her list. Casey raised an eyebrow.

"And that Mary asked for money," Kate added. She leaned forward to look at Casey better in the dim light. She was trying to read his expression.

Casey scowled. "Did he say if he had given an answer?"

"He said that they agreed that the baby would not know his real father."

"So, Gardner and Greco are corroborating each other's stories. Good. But, did one of them kill her?" Casey squinted his eyes, trying to find holes in the stories.

Betty tried picturing the stories also. "Well, Tony said he waited til almost dark for Mary to come back. Then he went home. Took the Green Line from Park Station to, probably North Station, then walked the rest of the way to his place."

"And," pointed out Kate, "Gardner says that he left her behind at the Gardens."

"Didn't Greco say he watched Mary chase after Gardner?" Casey asked, looking at his notebook.

"Wait! If Mary chased after Gardner and Tony walked around the Gardens til almost 9, then Mary either did not stay in the Gardens like Gardner says or did not return to the Gardens like Tony said. Either way, I don't think she was in the Gardens that late. Yet, that bar from the swan boat seems to be the murder weapon and it certainly was in the Gardens." Betty was alternately looking at each hand, weighing the evidence, so to speak.

Casey closed his eyes and leaned back in the chair. "If she did not go back to the house nor return to the Gardens, what could she have been doing? I don't see her taking the trolley to Greco's place at night. She would have had to have some work ethic for Mrs. Milton to keep her. She would not have bothered to not return on time. That would be grounds for dismissal."

"Do you think she may have been restrained from returning?" Kate asked, surprised that she realized the possibility. Her eyes opened wide at the thought.

Casey sat up in his chair and leaned towards her. "That is exactly what I am thinking. The problem is who. Our two leading suspects seem to be innocent of the crime, for now."

The sisters looked at one another. "Harold?" The older man did not seem a likely candidate for striking a woman hard enough to kill her.

Casey groaned. "He doesn't seem the type. But, what do I know? Rich people tend to make their employees dependent on them for their lives. This old guy has been working for Mrs. Milton since the Titanic went down. He supports them completely. Who knows? Enough emotion or fear of rocking the boat and he may have the strength." He looked at his watch. "It is almost 11. I don't know how you two have so much energy, but I put in a full day and I would just as soon wrap up this little party." He put his hand over Kate's. "I know this was not exactly the kind of date that a girl thinks of," he added apologetically.

"That's all right. I expected something like this." She put her free hand over his and smiled.

"So, what are you going to do now?" Betty interjected.

Casey rubbed his forehead. "I am booked tomorrow. So, I am going to call on the Miltons first thing the next morning. Probably early enough for a fresh cup of coffee."

"But that is Saturday. You don't usually work on Saturdays," Kate objected.

"That is why it's special. The banks aren't open on Saturdays. Mr. Milton may be around. I have not written him off, yet." He winked at her, then got up from the table.

"Why Mr. Milton?" Kate asked as the sisters grabbed their purses and got off their chairs.

"It is a long shot, but with the money this guy has, protecting it under every circumstance is a possible motive."

The three moved towards the door, fighting the late-night crowd trying to get in. They looked around for Jonathan, to thank him for setting up the meeting with Tony Greco. But he was too busy and all they could do was wave to him.

SATURDAY MORNING

It was barely 8 am when the phone rang next to Kate's bedside table. She rubbed her eyes and stared at the jangling phone for a moment before she got her wits about her. She reached over the pillows and grabbed the sleek white receiver then laid back down.

"Hello?" Her voice was husky from sleep.

"Miss Kate, it is Lt. Roach," James's voice informed her.

"Thank you, James. I will take it." Kate waited to hear the click before beginning. "Casey! Why are you calling so early?"

"I wanted to share a piece of information with you before I stopped over at the Martins."

"I hope it is important. I was having a very nice dream."

"It may be a very odd coincidence, but maybe not. Since you and Betty are so involved, I thought your advice would be appreciated."

Kate sat up and swallowed hard. "Well, if I can give you any advice, I would love to!" She put her fingers through her shoulder length curls, as if to look a little better. Then she snuggled into the pillows, again.

"I had to step into the office this morning. There was a note on my desk. It was from Jonathan, the maître d' at the Grove."

"What was so important?"

"You know the Grove is not known for its honesty in business, right?"

"I read the papers, Casey!"

"Well, it seems that, by sheer coincidence," Casey coughed. "Tony was offered the job at the Grove the day after the murder."

"I can see that. He said he was looking for jobs when we went to his place, asking questions."

"But that is not all. Jonathan says Mr. Milton called Barney Welansky, the owner, asking him to quickly find a place for a kid. Jonathan says that Milton and Welansky have some ties. The kid is Tony Greco."

Kate bolted upright.. "Oh, my! That is quite a coincidence!"

"So, you just answered my question. Thanks, Kate. I am on my way over to the Miltons, now."

"Casey!" Kate's throat was tight. "Be safe, please. This is a little scary."

"Don't worry about me, Kate. Talk to you soon." Casey hung up on his end. Kate just looked at her receiver and bit her lower lip.

After a few moments, Kate hung up and got out of bed. She put on a dressing gown and brushed her hair. She opened the door and went down the hall to Betty's room. Knocking softly, she walked into the room. Betty was already awake, sitting up in bed with arms folded.

"Who calls the house at 8am on a Saturday?" Betty complained.

"It was Casey."

"Why?"

"Jonathan, the maitre d' at the Grove called the police station looking for Casey. Someone wrote out a note for him and put it on Casey's desk. Apparently, Mr. Milton knows Barney Welansky. And," Kate dropped her voice. "He asked for a favor from Welansky! He wanted a kid to get a job, immediately. That kid is Tony!"

"That is a little too coincidental, don't you think?" Betty's eyes got wide.

"That's what I said."

"Do you think his telling you all this is illegal? What is Casey going to do?"

"No. He is fine about telling us," Kate brushed it off. "By the way, he is on his way over to the Miltons, now. I am going to get dressed and eat early. I am sure Casey will want to tell us something after his interview."

"If things go well…"

Kate looked at Betty with some angst and left the room.

Two hours went by very slowly. Kate sat on the window seat in the breakfast room, nursing her third cup of coffee. Betty paced the room. The police vehicle had been parked outside the Martin home for an hour and a half.

"Do you think they have told him the whole story?" Kate asked impatiently.

"I am wondering about our neighbors, truly. I thought that Evelyn was a nice, plain Brahmin with her nose in the air. And I thought she had a cute son. And I knew that Mr. Milton is the president of the Federal Reserve," Betty began, pacing in time to her words. "Then I find out Evelyn is very eccentric, Charles fools around with maids and gets them into trouble and Mr. Milton knows gangsters enough to ask favors." She looked thoughtfully at her sister, hands on her hips. "Do you know, I never imagined a gangster type living right next door!"

"I hope Mr. Milton is not really a gangster type," Kate responded. "I wish I was with the police

department. Then I could be there with Casey,

hearing the conversation."

Betty turned suddenly in her pacing. "We can eavesdrop!"

"How?"

Betty approached her sister and looked down at her. "Let's go see how the Miltons' cook is doing? After all, her world has been turned upside down. She may be suffering. We know her, right? We should be good neighbors!"

Kate's eyes grew large. She put down her coffee cup and stood. "The only thing I have to say is, why didn't I think of that earlier?" She headed for the hallway. "Are you coming?" She ran to the front hall, stopping only long enough to check her lipstick. Then they both ran out the back, kitchen door, waving to Sally and Cook.

When they got to the common courtyard for the block, they went down along the stone wall that was the demarcation of the property line. At the back of the Milton house, they rang the bell at the delivery entrance. Mrs. Kelly answered immediately. She must have been just the other side of the door.

"Oh, Misses Hadley! I am so glad to see you!" she nearly cried. Opening the door wider, she added, "Please come in."

The young ladies noticed her heaving chest and

on the uniform chest. "What is going on, Mrs. Kelly? The police have been here a long time." The older woman put her finger to her lips then guided them through the kitchen and into her sitting room before saying another word. She sat in her rocker and picked up yesterday's newspaper to fan herself. "I would not believe it myself, if I hadn't heard it." She rocked and fanned without another word for a minute.

The sisters could not hear anything from their position on the loveseat. The house was actually well sound-proofed between the kitchen and the owners' living quarters. They looked at each other and shrugged, neither knowing quite what to expect.

Finally, Mrs. Kelly opened her eyes and stared at the two visitors. "I have worked for Mrs. Milton for ten years. She was a widow when I came to be with her and her son was a precocious lad of thirteen. He left for Oxford, and then she remarried. It was a quiet life. Now, the boy returns as a man and it turns out that Mrs. Milton cannot raise a gentleman nor marry one!" She groaned and closed her eyes. The rocking and fanning began again.

"Mrs. Kelly! You really must tell me what is going on!" Kate insisted.

"That poor girl! She was put upon by that young upstart, Mr. Gardner. He admitted it to the police lieutenant! What a terrible thing he did!" The

97

fanning increased in ferocity.

Betty nodded. She looked down at her hands, embarrassed to have this conversation with the poor woman. "We knew," she uttered quietly.

"And Mr. Milton knows mobsters!" the older woman threw her hands in the air, in a sign of despair, the newspaper flying across the room. "I can hardly be expected to cook for mobsters coming to the house!" she added in a shaky voice.

Kate leaned forward. "What do the mobsters have to do with the police coming over?" she asked innocently.

Mrs. Riley stopped rocking. She looked at them seriously. "I don't know. I had to start lunch. I thought you might know something."

A bang on the swinging kitchen door caused the older woman to jump up and race from her room. The girls followed behind, but stopped short at her suite door when they saw Harold, the butler come in with a silver tray.

"They ask for more tea, Kelly," he noted.

"Why don't those police just stop the questioning and arrest someone!" Mrs. Kelly snapped.

"Oh, the police are wrapping up. It's the Missus who needs the tea." He put the dirty cups into the sink and pulled another two out of the cabinets.

"Have you got those sandwiches made?" he asked as he scanned the kitchen countertops.

"How is the Missus?" the cook asked, pulling a complete dish of sandwiches from the refrigerator and putting it on the tray.

"I am surprised she hasn't passed out," Harold reported. "I informed her Master Charles told me the situation that night."

"You knew?" Cook almost dropped the tea kettle she had just picked up. "You didn't tell me!" she added accusingly.

"Madam! You can hardly blame me if that child told me something in confidence." He picked up the hot kettle and filled the teapot himself. Then he left the kitchen.

Mrs. Kelly turned back to the Hadleys. "I might have been able to figure this out if I had known days ago, rather than this morning!" She was now incensed.

Betty looked at Kate. "How much of the situation did Charles tell Harold? Did Charles end up going back and killing her? Did Harold?"

"Well, someone killed that poor child!"

They heard the front door shut with a bang.

"That will be the police!" Betty said as she quickly

crossed the kitchen. Kate followed right behind. "We will see if we can get something out of them!"

They ran around the corner of the house and saw Casey and Perkins standing outside the police unit. The two slowed down and tried to look like they just happened to be walking along the sidewalk. Casey saw them and looked at them sourly.

"Trying to eavesdrop?" he asked with a scowl.

Kate looked sheepish. "I heard that Mrs. Kelly was a little under the weather."

He raised his eyebrows. "I am supposed to believe that," he snapped. "Have you any words of wisdom before I leave?"

Kate was a little taken aback by his attitude. She thought he was stressed by the last few days' events. "Mrs. Kelly didn't know until today that Mary was definitely expecting or that Charles had been the father. Harold knew but did not tell her."

"Well, that's not all Harold knew," Casey mumbled. He turned and got into the passenger's seat in the big car. Kate approached but he waved her off and Perkins gunned the accelerator to leave.

"What did I do?" Kate looked up at Betty in surprise.

"I think maybe he can't divulge a police investigation."

Elizabeth A Martina

"But we were with him at the Grove when he questioned Tony."

"I think he may have gotten something big in that questioning, my dear sister. Something that will lead to an answer. And he has to do it quickly."

"I hate when he gets too far ahead of us!" Kate pouted. "And I hate knowing that there have potentially been mobsters around the neighborhood and I didn't get to see!" She kicked a stone with her foot and it flew into the street.

"Look. It is noon. Let's get some lunch and calm down. We can plan our afternoon." Betty tugged at Kate's arm and they silently returned to the house.

Over a shrimp salad and a dessert of chocolate mousse, Kate calmed down and thought rationally about Casey's apparent attitude.

"Let's go over all the possible murderers," Betty introduced as she placed down her spoon. "It is not likely to be Charles. He is a deviant little boy, but hardly one to get his hands dirty."

Kate looked up. "That is right. He wears white, like a proper Newport summer resident. I can't see his ruining his clothes or changing, if he had a date at the same time."

"So, there is Harold, the butler. Could he have done it? I doubt it."

"That's right. Look at him. A milquetoast. He would not be likely to grab a big piece of metal and swing it, much less want to kill someone. But he is very loyal to Mrs. Milton, and, I assume, to Mr. Milton."

Betty got up from the table and began to pace. Her best thinking was whenever she paced. "Now, we know that Mr. Milton knew about Tony, because of Jonathan's letter. Wonder why he went out of his way to try to get the poor fellow a job"

Kate stared into the distance for a minute, trying to picture the way the eyes of Tony Greco shifted as he spoke to them Thursday night. "Two possibilities there. Number one, Milton felt sorry for Tony and got him a job out of the kindness of his heart in the days before the murder. Tony had been out of a job for a week before that, remember."

Betty turned to look at her sister. "And the other?"

"Payback for something."

"Any other possible choice?" Betty asked. "I kind of like the poor man." She started pacing again.

Kate went back to staring into space as she sorted out other possibilities. She turned to Betty and shook her head. "Not that I can see."

"So, we need to find out when Mr. Milton called Welansky and asked for the favor," Betty pointed out.

"Well, that is easy. Remember what Tony said at the Grove? The morning we went to find him, he was dressing for the interview. So, the morning after the murder." Kate stopped. "Or the night of?" She shuddered at the thought.

"That means, probably," Betty analyzed. "That either he saw something someone wants him to forget or he is getting paid for something he did."

"That doesn't make sense. Not if he was getting paid to kill the girl he was sweet on. If I was he, and I killed the girl of my dreams, I would head out West where no one could find me." Kate toyed with her napkin, frustrated.

"You have been watching too many movies, my dear!" Betty quipped. "But I have to agree with you. Killing a girl and sticking around to get a low paying job just doesn't make sense."

"So, we are left with the assumption that Tony saw something he shouldn't have and they are paying him off to keep quiet." Kate put her chin on her hand and studied the wall. "I cannot come up with another idea."

Betty came back to the table and sat down. "You know. I just had a nasty thought. Mary was placed in a basement near Tony's place. Do you think that is added insurance that Tony keep quiet? It would

be easy enough to plant another piece of incrim-
inating evidence around there to prove that it was
Tony all along, assuming he tells someone."

Kate sat back in her chair, stunned at the thought.
"Oooh, that is nasty. And very possible!"

"So, dear sister, how do we proceed?" Betty got that
look in her eye when she was ready to get up and
run.

Sally walked into the room to clean the dishes off
the table. "Do you mind if I clean around you two
detectives," she grinned. "I've been overhearing
you."

"Sally, we need to ask Tony what really happened.
But if we question him again, he will get suspicious
and keep quiet." Betty had a wild look in her eyes.
She had an idea.

"Oh, Miss Hadley! You have a scheme. I can tell."

Betty pulled out the chair next to her own. "Sit
down, Sally. I have an idea. And you can get paid
for it."

It was 9:00 pm. Kate and Betty had not heard from
Casey. They had gone to a band concert on the
Common and had just returned. The two ran up to
the third floor of the house, where the three staff
members lived, and knocked on Sally's door. She

opened the door, dressed in a summer weight dress of blue, trimmed in black, with black pumps and purse.

"You look great, Sally!" Betty exclaimed. "Without the cap, your hair is so wavy. Just lovely!"

Kate nudged her sister in the ribs. "Hush! You don't want Cook to know what is going on!"

Sally chuckled quietly. "I just called a taxi."

"James and Cook didn't hear, did they?"

"I doubt it. I used the phone in the kitchen. Then I came back up here to wait for you."

Betty opened her purse and handed Sally a $20 bill. "Here. You will have to spend some money before you get his attention. Are you fine with the plan?"

"I am, Miss Betty. I have invented a whole storyline." Sally smiled a little tremulously as she tucked the bill into her small purse. "I will be fine."

"Well, you had better get downstairs before the taxi comes. We don't want James to run down two flights and find out our plans." Betty patted Sally's arm.

They walked down the two flights together, just in time to see the taxi drive up. Sally began her venture.

SUNDAY MORNING

It was two am when a weary Sally walked through the front door of the house. Both Betty and Kate were still up, waiting for her to come home, like an anxious mother whose daughter was on her first date.

The sisters, both in their dressing gowns, raced out of Kate's room, where they had been occupying themselves, trying to stay awake. They met Sally at the top of the stairs, anxious for news.

"Did you see him?"

"Did you get a chance to talk to him at length?"

"What did he say?"

Questions tumbled over one another in hushed voices as they followed Sally up to her room. The maid kicked her pumps off once she entered her room and sunk down on the edge of the bed.

"I would rather serve a party single-handedly than do that again!" she proclaimed. "I don't see how you can talk to people as long as you do!"

Her bosses laughed. "But did you get any information?"

"Tony is really a sweet guy," Sally went to the mirrored bureau and began to explain as she brushed out her hair and took off her borrowed jewelry. "He is totally heartbroken about Mary. There is no way he could have killed her. Just like you said." The sisters nodded to each other, in silent congratulations over their assumption being verified.

"I played the poor girl who lost her man," Sally explained. "Just like you instructed. I am a pretty good actress!" She beamed with self-confidence.

"How did you run into him?" Betty wanted the facts.

"I told the maître d' that I had just lost my fiancé and wanted a bus boy who would be able to cater to me and understand my loss."

"That is quite the request! And it worked?"

"It was amazing! The maître d' found me a small table for two in a corner and turned off the spotlight. He put a candle on the table and told Tony to help me with whatever I would need." Sally sat on the edge of the bed again.

"Did Tony act suspicious?" Kate asked. She had not been sure that this long shot would work at all.

"Not a bit. I started talking about my 'loss' and he started to talk about his. I told him how my fiancé had died in a shootout and he told how his girlfriend had been bludgeoned to death."

"How does he know that?" Kate blurted out. Sally looked at the two quizzically.

Betty explained. "The cause of death was not in the newspapers and I know he did not get to see the autopsy report. You have to be next of kin for that."

Sally's eyes opened wide. "He had to talk to someone who saw it, or he saw it, himself!"

"Exactly!" the two sisters responded in unison.

"So, did you two talk about anything else?" Betty asked.

"He told me the murder was in the Garden. That the two had met there at night to plan their lives together. He said she was expecting another man's child and that this man would pay for her to keep quiet. They were going to elope."

"That is a different story from the one he told us," Betty pointed out. "He said that he left the Gardens and took a trolley to the North End."

Sally shrugged her shoulder. "I started crying over my man who had died and he started crying over Mary. Then, after he stopped, he put his hands over mine and made me swear that I would not tell a soul. Because he was told that, should he tell someone, his life was doomed."

Kate cringed. She gulped hard. "Did he see it happen?"

Sally thought back on the conversation they had had. "I don't think he actually did. They were walking through the Gardens, near the swan boats. It was dark. Probably after nine, then. They heard banging sounds and turned around to see two dark figures actually pounding on one of the boats. Then one of the figures had a stick in his hand. It was dull red, Tony said, because he saw the reflection from one of the path lights around the pond."

"He actually told you all this?" Kate asked, shocked at the detail.

Sally nodded. "He was crying. He was feeling guilty, I would assume. He couldn't tell anyone except me, a total unknown, who would disappear in an hour."

"Did anyone overhear you two talking?" Betty leaned forward in the small straight chair.

"I don't think so. I played that I was a wreck and just wanted to be in the place where my fiancé and I had our last date. I begged for privacy."

"You are a good actress!" Kate said admiringly. "Did he tell you more?"

"He said that the figures started to walk towards them and he and Mary began to run. The figures ran towards them. Mary ran around one side of a bush and Tony, the other. Tony said he was ahead of her and turned around to grab her when she stumbled.

The figures were catching up. Tony got scared and started running towards the Common. He heard one scream. He didn't dare turn back because he heard one of the figures racing towards him. He could hear the man's heavy breathing as he got to Park Station." Sally paused to picture what he told her. "You know how that station is always busy til almost midnight, what with all the theaters and shows along Tremont. Tony said he ducked into the crowd, just ahead of the man and lost him."

Kate shook her head sadly, with a look of disgust on her face.

"So, the figure who, presumably, chased him is not the person who warned Tony," Betty surmised.

"No. He said that he had a visitor to his rooms the next afternoon."

"So, after we were there. I guess he really was out job searching in the morning."

"The guy knew who he was and where he had worked. The fellow offered him a job at the Grove, if he could keep his mouth shut, or that's how Tony told it." Sally yawned. "Can we continue this in the morning? I am so exhausted. And I have to be up in five hours."

"Oh, certainly! I am sorry, Sally, but this is so fascinating!" Kate felt bad using Sally so much. "How about I put a note on Cook's door and tell her you can start at 8, because it is Sunday and no one is getting up early?"

"Thank you, Miss Kate." Sally stood to walk the sisters to the door. "I must admit, it is fun doing detective work with you two."

Kate turned back to Sally. "Someday, we should have a business!" Then she laughed and left.

When Kate and Betty got down to the second floor, Betty turned to her sister. "How are we going to handle this news with Casey?"

"I don't know. I could say I just lent a dress, shoes and jewelry to our maid and she ran into Tony at the Grove. But somehow, I don't think he would believe me."

"Not for a moment!"

"It is late. I will think of how to handle him in the morning. Good night, Betty!"

After church, Betty, Kate and Dr. Hadley sat down to lunch. Hadley had been very busy with a paper he had been writing, to the point that he had been in his office at Harvard the past two days and had returned late every night. He made it a point to try to catch up on the end of the week events.

"Have you made any headway with this mystery of

yours?" Hadley asked as he placed his linen napkin on his lap. "Obviously, there was no problem at the Grove."

"We saw that Lt. Roach went over to the Miltons' yesterday morning. But he did not have a chance to talk to us, yet."

"No call last night?"

Kate blushed. "No. I think he was busy."

"Well, then, I think it is a good idea that he is coming over this afternoon."

Kate looked up from her soup, in surprise. "He is?" She looked at her father's steady blue eyes. "How do you know that?"

"I personally called his office on Friday and told him it was time we met. I invited him over at 3:00."

Kate put down her soup spoon and looked at him in shock.

Then she reached over and grabbed his unoccupied left hand. "Oh, Dad! That is so kind of you!"

"Kind?" the blue eyes twinkled. "It is more likely a necessity! You have been seeing him for months and have not given me any clues except a name. Even if he is Irish, I should meet him. You never know. He could become family someday." His bushy eyebrows hid his eyes as he looked down at his soup, avoiding what could be an emotional gaze.

Kate patted his hand and turned her attention back to her soup. She would see Casey, after all, this weekend.

"And what did you do yesterday while I was writing?" Hadley asked as he pushed his empty bowl away.

"We had a quiet day. Sat around in the morning and went to an evening concert at the Music Hall."

"Some Beethoven and Bach, perhaps?"

"And Paderewski."

Dr. Hadley looked approvingly at his two daughters and nodded. "We need more of this and less of that jazz stuff. I admit that some, like Gershwin, in his short life, were quite talented, but I can barely stand to listen to the stuff for more than a minute. Discordant." He shook his head, then leaned back for Sally to put a large piece of prime roast in front of him.

Kate and Betty smiled to themselves, glad that he accepted their story of a quiet day. Casey would hear all the facts at 3.

Shortly before 3pm, Casey's green Opel Cabriolet pulled up to the curb. When he stepped out of the car, he was dressed impeccably in a windowpane plaid jacket, white flannel pants, a black shirt with white tie. His white buckskin shoes looked expensive for a poor police lieutenant. Casey was putting on a decided front for Dr. Hadley.

James let Casey in as the family waited in the professor's study. Kate stood ready to welcome him in, smoothing her green crepe skirt of its invisible wrinkles. Casey, all smiles, walked over to her first, kissed her cheek then turned to her father.

"Dr. Hadley, I am pleased to meet you, finally." Casey extended his arm and in two steps, he was at Hadley's side.

"The pleasure is mine, sir." The professor took Casey's hand and shook it. He motioned to a matching chair next to his own and Casey took it. Kate sat on the arm of Casey's chair. Betty went to a table containing a tray of bottles and glasses to mix some drinks.

"Have you tried a Boston Side Car, Casey?" she asked. Casey raised one eyebrow and shook his head. "Then you have to try it," she said, handing a glass to him. "Brandy, lime juice, triple sec and white rum. Shaken." She smiled as he sipped it, then nodded approvingly. After she had handed the drinks out, Betty sat near her father.

Dr. Hadley took a sip and placed the glass on the end table between the two matching chairs. "I am most interested in how your investigation has gone regarding the murder of that poor child who was working next door."

Casey put his drink down and leaned forward. "The latest will be in tomorrow's papers except for one thing: The name of the fellow who actually did it. It was quite a well-planned setup."

Hadley was stunned. "You mean this girl was murdered by plan?"

"Well, you see, sir. Your young neighbor does not seem to have much self-control and takes what he wants, when he wants it. So, he took what he wanted with the maid, if I make myself clear."

"Perfectly. The young man should be in jail."

"It is rather a moot point at this time, since we cannot ask her if she consented. She was 17." Casey took another sip from his glass and licked his lips. "When she realized the situation she was in, she had already gotten herself a boyfriend. And within a short period of time, she apparently resolved to give her child a name. She convinced the boyfriend to marry her and raise the child as his own. But, since he was jobless and she would soon forfeit her job, they needed money."

"Ah, blackmail?" the older man suggested.

"No, apparently, they were fairly honorable. They asked Charles Gardner. Or, rather, I believe Mary asked, on her own. Gardner apparently thought he might do something. But, what, we do not know. He says he planned on offering them two thousand. At any rate, the couple had a little run in with Gardner the night it happened and there were some punches thrown and Gardner's jacket ripped. He had to go home to change for a date."

Sally brought in a tray of appetizers and passed them around. She put the half empty tray on an end table and left, keeping the study door ajar.

"Apparently, Harold, the butler, was quite close to Gardner before he went to Oxford. He wanted the story of how a perfectly good jacket could rip. So, Gardner explained the circumstances. Well, Harold, being the very loyal butler that he is, told Mr. Milton since he was home from work. Harold even mentioned why Mary wanted the money. Milton had a fit and decided to rid himself of the problem."

"Are you saying that George Milton killed his own maid?" Dr.

Hadley gasped. Betty and Kate exchanged glances. This did not match what Tony had told Sally.

"Not exactly. I am pretty sure he didn't do it, personally. After questioning those people yesterday, I am sure that Milton spent the evening at home. Evelyn Milton swears she and her husband had eaten a late supper then spent the evening listening to chamber music on the radio. Harold swears he spoke to Mr. Milton at 8:pm or just after." Casey shrugged. "They did not seem to be lying. And I really can't pin anything on anyone. I don't know where to go from here." He took another sip from his glass.

Kate put her arm around Casey and looked down at him. She took a deep breath. "Casey, dear, I have a bit more information."

He glanced up at her. "What have you been up to, this time?"

Dr. Hadley started. He glared at Kate then turned to Betty. "Are you two in to something I would not approve of?" Casey looked at Betty sternly.

Betty grinned sheepishly. "It was Kate's idea."

Sally walked into the room to remove the appetizer tray. It was still half full. No one spoke, waiting for her to leave. She didn't and took up a position behind Betty's chair.

"You are not needed, Sally" Hadley said gruffly.

"Oh, yes, she is," Betty immediately retorted.

"Are you in on this too?" Casey asked, looking into Sally's eyes. She blushed. "Oh, for heaven's sake!" he added when he saw this. Casey picked up his glass and downed the rest of the contents then placed it down again. "All right. I am ready." He looked up at Kate's face. She was biting her lower lip, trying to compose herself.

"We thought we could help you," Kate began. "You seemed so upset when you left the Miltons' the other afternoon."

"You sat around all day, eh?" interjected her father.

She ignored him. "I developed a brilliant idea and it worked!" Casey looked at her, afraid of her next words.

"I lent some clothes to Sally. That is not hard. She and I are the same size. And she went to the Grove. She ran into Tony and he told her everything."

"And how is it that she just so happened to get him to tell her everything, as you say?"

Sally blurted out, "I am a very good actress!"

Casey groaned. "What did you do?"

"I went to the Grove and told the maître d' that I had recently lost my fiancé and wanted to sit in the same place where we had had our last date. There is a little alcove with a spotlight, a ways away from the dance floor. Then I said I only wanted someone to serve me who understood loss. It worked out perfectly!"

"Did Jonathan know who you were?" Casey cringed at the thought.

"The maître d'? No."

Casey closed his eyes and leaned back his head. No one said a word. Kate looked down at him, watching his eyes flit back and forth beneath his lids. He was trying to picture what he had just heard. After thirty seconds or so, he opened his eyes and asked her to go on.

"Well, I turned on the waterworks, sobbing and drying my eyes every time he came by. Eventually, he sat down and asked if he could help. So, I made up a story about how my fiancé had died trying to stop a burglary. I did really good. I was sniffing and blabbering the whole time. So, then, he started crying and said practically the same thing happened to him. And his fiancée died." She described the whole scene, just as she told the sisters the night before.

"I am getting the idea that the death of Mary has nothing to do with the Miltons, after all." Casey began to rub his head. "This is giving me a headache."

"So, the two people vandalizing the swan boat are the likely cause of the murder. But how does that explain why Milton asked Welansky to get Tony a job?" Betty insisted.

"Welansky? How would a man like George Milton know a mobster like Barney Welansky?" Dr.

Hadley got up from his chair and turned to Casey. "Are you putting my daughters in danger, Lt. Roach?"

"Excuse me, sir. But everyone who is someone in downtown Boston knows Mr. Welansky and his 'acquaintances'. A lawyer like Welansky needs a bank, as well, remember."

"Hmph. Ill-gotten gains!" Hadley turned up his nose and returned to his seat.

Casey sat mulling over the last few comments. "We need the answer to another question before I am satisfied that we have it right. Why move the body, if the murderer was a simple vandal? It was done almost immediately, according to the coroner."

"So, Casey, what do we do next?" Kate asked.

He looked at her wryly. "I think you have done enough." He laughed at himself and patted her hand. "Actually, if it were not for you, we would never have gotten this far this fast." He looked over to Betty and Sally and nodded. "And the same to you two. Thank you."

"If only we could figure out what was the purpose in Mr. Milton calling for a favor," Kate reflected.

"I am going to have to excuse myself," Casey announced, rising from his seat. "I need to ask that very question to your neighbor this afternoon. And a few more. I won't be able to sleep tonight without it."

Kate got off the arm of the chair and looked up at him. "I am sorry to have you leave so soon. Could you, perhaps, come back afterwards?"

Casey kissed her. "No, I don't think so. I will have to spend the evening rewriting my report to the chief and adding the new information I will get from Milton. I believe he is home. There has been a car parked in front of the house since I got here." He put his hand on her shoulder. "I will call you tonight." He bent and kissed her again.

He pivoted to Dr. Hadley and extended his hand. "It has been a pleasure meeting you, sir. I hope to do it again under better circumstances." They shook hands.

"Yes. Perhaps we can do this again, soon," the older gentleman assured Casey.

Turning to Betty and Sally, he grinned at them. "I do hope you two realize that I am the police and you are not." He shook his head. "You did well this time. But, please realize that this is dangerous activity at times. You don't want to get hurt! Thank you, though." Grabbing his fedora, he left the room, Sally following to close the front door.

"I suppose we will have to wait a few days before we get more information," Betty said dismally.

"I am getting anxious to put this behind us," Kate responded. "It has been almost a week and we still don't have a why." She sat back on the chair still warm from Casey. "If we know why Mary was killed, then we will know why and who transported the body." She sighed. "Maybe."

Casey's adrenaline was racing through his veins by the time he reached the Miltons' front door. He pressed the doorbell hard and searched his pockets for a writing utensil and some paper, which he always brought with him. Harold answered the door.

"Oh, are you here again, Lieutenant? I thought we had answered all your questions yesterday."

"I am sorry to bother Mr. Milton again, Harold. But I need a few things wrapped up before I can make an arrest. And my boss does not like waiting too long for me to figure things out. May I?"

Casey had his foot on the threshold and Harold could not shut the door. It opened wider and Casey walked onto the parquet floors of the foyer. He turned into the obnoxiously decorated receiving room immediately, assuming Harold would find Mr. Milton for him. It being 4pm on a Sunday, Casey could not think of an excuse that Milton could come up with.

However, George Milton was not going to jump up from what he was doing and greet Casey immediately. The young lieutenant sat doodling on his notepad for twenty minutes before the banker showed his perturbed face. Still wearing his business suit, he walked in, alone.

"What do you need now, lieutenant?" the grey-haired gentleman asked in the least welcoming way possible. He stood by the door to the foyer, unwilling to come further in.

Casey stood immediately. "I went over a few notes I took yesterday, Mr. Milton. And I want to clarify a few things." He held up his well-used notepad.

Martin made no pretext of hospitality. He looked at his watch. "I have a dinner engagement at 6. My wife has no intentions of our not going." He looked up at the young man and crossed his arms.

Casey took a deep breath. "I am sure I can accommodate you. Just a few questions. Would you like to sit?"

"No." He did not move.

Casey shrugged his shoulders. He had tried polite. "You contacted Barney Welansky late last Tuesday night or early Wednesday morning. Yes?"

Martin stood like a statue and did not respond.

"I happen to know from good sources that this is

true." Casey paused. "What is the relationship you have with Barney Welansky?"

Martin's eyes grew wide. But just for a moment. He gained control of himself and gritted his teeth. "I work with him as part of a legal team."

"For the bank?"

"NO."

"For personal purposes, then." Casey deliberately wrote on his notebook. "And, how is it that Tony Greco is a personal purpose of yours?"

Milton's face paled. His hand went up to the doorjamb and his knees started to buckle. Casey threw down his notebook and rushed to Milton's side. Grabbing the older man, he walked him to the closest chair and sat him down.

"Put your head down and don't move," he ordered his host.

Then he ran out to the foyer and called for Harold, who appeared instantly. "A glass of water for Mr. Milton, Harold!" Casey went back in to attend the older man. Harold reappeared with water and a small pill. Glancing down, Casey saw that it was a nitroglycerin tablet.

It took only a few moments for the nitro to start working. Color came back into the older man's face and he sat back in the chair, breathing normally.

Casey brought another chair up to face the man. "Heart condition, right?"

Martin nodded. "Harold knows. But Evelyn, she doesn't understand. I tell her it is a painkiller for arthritis." He smiled wryly.

"I can come back another time, sir. I didn't mean to get you that upset."

Milton looked him in the eye. "I am not getting better, Lieutenant. I probably don't have much time left. This thing has ruined my heart." He shook his head. "I have no children of my own. Evelyn had Charles, but he was away at Oxford when we married. I really don't know how to handle children, even one with a bachelor's degree." He looked at Casey, silently asking for understanding.

"What does that have to do with my question?"

"Only that I knew about Charles' little difficulty." Casey lifted one eyebrow. "He takes all the girls he can. I thought we had him on a short leash here, but I thought wrong."

Casey nodded, knowingly.

"When Harold told me last Tuesday night, I blew a gasket. I wasn't going to let some little minx from Ireland inherit all Evelyn's money. Harold told me that she wanted money. You know with that kind. You give them a few thousand and a few years

later, they have gone through that and want more!"
Milton sat back for a moment, catching his breath.

"I assume you did not trust her word?" Casey asked.

"You don't trust the Irish. I don't care if Honey Fitz
is talking about taking the Senate seat. Irish is Irish,
shanty or lace curtain."

"I am Irish."

"You'll do for now," Martin said with a wave of his
hand. "I wasn't going to pay for her antics with
Charles for the next 21 years!" That last was said
almost pleadingly.

"What did you do, Mr. Milton?"

"I called my lawyer. I asked him if he could handle
the situation. I thought something like rescind her
work visa or convince her to move to Texas or
somewhere. That is not my forte. I do numbers."

"Is that all you two said to each other?"

"He said it would be best for me to call Bernie
Welansky. He has an associate who could take care
of things right away. So, I called Welansky and
gave him the story. I told him that she had not come
home at 7 and that, with any luck, she may have run
away and this is all for nothing."

"Did he ask anything, like where did she go?"

"No, I don't think so." Martin said slowly. "No.

Wait. I did mention that she was seen near the swan boats before 8. It was just before then that the altercation with Charles and her boyfriend occurred."

"I know." Casey was trying to be as compassionate as possible while furiously writing down, in a form of shorthand, every word. "So, I have one more question for you, Mr. Milton: Did you call Mr. Welansky the next day and ask him to get a job for Tony Greco?"

Martin closed his eyes and leaned back in the chair. His fingers curled around the upholstered edges of the chair, his fingers digging into the pristine material. Then his shoulders dropped and he sat back up. "I made a terrible mistake. Asking Welansky to solve my problem." He shook his head and rubbed his eyes with the palm of his hands.

"Mr. Milton, did you call Mr. Welansky the next day and ask him to get a job for Tony Greco?"

"Yes, I did. I had to do something for the poor kid." He leaned forward in the chair and covered his face with his hands.

"How did you get his name?"

Martin looked up at Casey and paused. "I asked the cook.

Cooks always know the gossip."

Casey half smiled, thinking of Kate and the way she got information. He bent his head down for a moment in an effort to hide his face. "Do you know that the young man was threatened?"

"Threatened?" It was obvious from the stunned look that Martin did not know this part of the story.

"He was told that if he ever spoke a word about what happened to Mary, that he would lose the job, or more." Casey watched Martin carefully.

Martin glared at Casey. "Are you trying to lead me on?"

"That is why I need to know who was the associate that Welansky got hold of. I need to question that fellow."

"Harold!" Martin bellowed. The butler arrived immediately.

"Get me Welansky at his home and bring the foyer phone in here when you get him."

"Certainly, sir!" the meek old man replied, and left.

The two men in the garish receiving room sat silently until Harold came back in, cord trailing along the floor. He handed the receiver to Martin and left the room, closing the pocket doors for privacy.

"Welansky? This is George Milton…..Thank you. I

have a question about last week's favor. The girl down by the Gardens. Who did you hire to solve that problem?......Where is he? I want to talk to him…..Are you kidding? …..Do you know where he found the kids who did the work? ......Who talked to the boy who got away?......No, eh?......No. I don't have any more questions. Thank you. ……. You have a nice evening as well." Martin hung up the phone and turned to Casey, who was still anxiously scribbling in the margins of his notebook.

"I don't have much, Lieutenant." Casey looked up at Martin. The man was being honest. "Welansky passed it off to a guy in his association. The guy had a heart attack two days ago and isn't talking at this point. The kids, who knows? A couple of kids from Dorchester, for all I know. He says that the kids didn't get the message about the level of violence. Everyone got scared. The kids called in a favor to hide the body. They got scared. The fact that it was found near the boyfriend is a sheer coincidence." He shrugged his shoulders. "I don't know. Welansky isn't known for his honesty."

"I thank you for making that call, sir," Casey immediately said, scribbling notes at the same time. "I am sure we won't be charging you with anything.

"I should have thought longer before I asked anyone for help." Martin said quietly. He watched Casey finish writing. "What is next?"

Casey closed his notebook. "I will wait and see if the associate recovers. If he does, I'll have a chance to question him. If not, I have no way of knowing where to look for those two boys. Tony won't get closure and life will go on." He stood up and looked at the mantle clock. "If you will excuse me, sir. I am invited for dinner."

Martin stood up and walked him to the front door. "I thank you for handling this. I wish, for the life of me, that I had never opened my mouth."

"It is behind us all, now, sir." Casey grabbed his fedora from the table in the foyer and walked out into the warm early evening air.

Casey walked over the small plot of grass to the house next door. Kate saw him come and ran to open the door for him.

"Are you finished?" she blurted. "Don't you have to go write up the report? Or call the police station?"

"The report can wait. I need a drink and then I am going to tell you the craziest end to a crazy story."

Elizabeth A Martina

Elizabeth wanted to be a writer from the age of seven. She wrote her first book in high school and, although it was never published, it already showed her interest in history. Since that time, she went on to various activities including homeschooling, teaching earth science, being a producer of a movie, republishing old books and fundraising for a water well project. She has two grown children, one lovable Bernese Mountain dog and an amazingly tolerant husband. Elizabeth is the product of early English immigrants and recent Italian immigrants. Her background includes a Mensa genius, the vice president of a railroad company, musicians, great cooks and a murderer, the subject of the book *The Ragman Murders*. Travel is in her bones as she has already traveled to Alaska, Japan, Europe and Uganda. Her latest bucket list wish, Uganda, was accomplished in 2019.

All authors are beholden to their readers for the books bought, appreciated and shared. Please spread the word by putting a review on the Amazon book page for this and all books that you enjoy. The authors will be grateful.